BOUN͟ BUTCHERBIRD

Gus Beaumont Thrillers
Book Three

Tony Rea

SAPERE
BOOKS

BOUNCER'S BUTCHERBIRD

Published by Sapere Books.

24 Trafalgar Road, Ilkley, LS29 8HH

saperebooks.com

ISBN: 978-0-85495-531-2

Dedicated to Able Seaman John Henry Cole, who was killed aboard HMS Hood *on 24th May 1941, aged 18.*

ACKNOWLEDGEMENTS

My heartfelt thanks go to my wife Jane for reading and critically commenting on the text. Thanks also to everyone at the Ivybridge Writers' Group. Their wise observations and valuable comments have strengthened the story enormously, and any mistakes remain my own. As always, Amy Durant and the team at Sapere Books have contributed their experience and professionalism. Thank you all.

PART ONE: THE SPECIAL OPERATIONS EXECUTIVE

CHAPTER 1

December 1941

Gus Beaumont hardly recognised his own reflection. His blue-grey RAF uniform was as smart as usual, but the face staring back at him didn't look like the face he remembered. It looked older, haggard even. His uniform had also changed. Gus held up a cuff and stared at the braids of a flight lieutenant it now sported; then he looked in the mirror again at the silk ribbon of the Distinguished Flying Cross above his left breast pocket.

Flight Lieutenant Gustaw Beaumont. Was that really him? He'd always been plain 'Bouncer' to the fellows in the mess. And to his friend Bunty Kermode, formerly of the Air Transport Auxiliary. She'd been badly injured in a crash-landing, and was out of action for the foreseeable future. Gus had had no correspondence from her in months and wondered how she was coping.

He thought he'd done little to deserve either his promotion or the DFC, apart from running errands for Wing Commander Sir Alexander Peacock. He'd been summoned to Peacock's office at 64 Baker Street soon after arriving home from the Mediterranean. The wing commander had told Gus of the promotion and medal. He had also offered Gus a posting to join 161 Squadron, a Special Operations Executive unit flying Westland Lysanders on secret night missions over occupied territory. If Gus was to take up Peacock's latest proposition, he needed to let him know soon. The war was changing, or at least he hoped so. Japan had attacked the US naval base at Pearl Harbor, and America was now fully committed to the war effort.

While he made his decision about what to do next, Gus was staying at his family home near Winchester. He descended the green-carpeted stairway and went into the study. There, he sat at the desk, held his head in his hands and closed his eyes. He wasn't fazed by flying a Lysander. He'd piloted these odd-looking, slow-moving aircraft before, at the start of the war. Nor did night flying present him with any particular concerns, since he'd had experience in Defiant and Hurricane night fighter squadrons.

Gus took some paper and a pen and began to write a letter to Wing Commander Peacock. He didn't get far. Just what was worrying him? Was it the thought of landing by moonlight in an isolated field in German-occupied France? Maybe, but this was war. Just about everything was dangerous. His friend Tunio Nowacki had been shot and killed by a Nazi pilot whilst dangling helplessly from a parachute over the Channel. Another friend, Spud Murphy, had burned to death trapped in the four-gun turret of a Boulton Paul Defiant. His first love Eunice Hesketh's parents had died in their own house when it was hit by Luftwaffe bombs.

Perhaps it was nothing to do with the job or even the war. His mother Magda's failing memory was a constant worry. A recent conversation with her had exposed the severity of her condition. They had been discussing Christmas preparations and his cousin's forthcoming visit. Magda had asked Gus to remind her when Stanislaw — she always used his full name — was due to visit.

"Christmas Eve," said Gus for the third time. "He can't get away any sooner."

"That's a shame," said Magda. "Still, it will be good to see him again." She paused, looking confused. "I last saw him at your father's funeral. That's right, isn't it?"

"Yes. But I've seen Staś since. I told you about it. Remember?"

"No. No, I don't recall. When did you see him last?"

"This year, just before I went to Greece."

"Greece!" Magda exclaimed. "But you haven't been to Greece, have you?" She wiped a tear from her eye and gazed at him sadly. "If only your father were still alive."

Gus saw that his mother had been confronted by her own frailty, and he couldn't think of anything to say. As she began to cry, he took her in his arms and held her close. Where this would end, he could not imagine. A posting to an RAF base in the Midlands or southern England would at least mean he might keep a closer eye on her — one reason for him to accept Peacock's offer.

As he recalled this distressing conversation, Gus poured a glass of sherry, penned the first line of his letter, then stopped again.

His thoughts had turned to Bunty Kermode. He'd met Bunty, an Air Transport Auxiliary pilot, when she'd delivered a Hurricane to the Polish squadron to which he'd been attached. She'd given a proper roasting to a young Polish pilot who'd dared to flirt with her. Gus had been impressed. Bunty, he thought, was quite unlike Eunice Hesketh. But every time he thought of Bunty, memories of Eunice clouded his mind.

They were two very different women. Eunice was complex and uncertain, whereas Bunty was confident, lively and gushing. Once he'd got used to Bunty's effusive ways, Gus had begun to think that her larger-than-life character was the more attractive, and she was great fun to be with. Anyway, he'd convinced himself that his relationship with Eunice was behind him.

He'd first met Eunice at Oxford before the war. They'd gone around together for a few months and then she'd finished it. What was it she'd told him? It wasn't a good time. Yes, that's what she said. But then she'd begun spending time with Murray Parkinson, though she insisted that nothing had happened between them. A couple of years after the end of their relationship, Eunice had told Gus that things had been getting too serious between them, so she'd picked up Murray at a party and hung out with him for a while, mostly to make sure Gus moved on.

Gus had bumped into Eunice again in London, at the beginning of the war. Later, she'd befriended Milly Turner — a young woman in the Women's Auxiliary Air Force — and the four of them, Eunice, Milly, Tunio and Gus had had a wonderful time. Until Eunice had left again, on the pretext of joining the Land Army and moving up to Scotland. Gus hadn't believed a word of it. Eunice had been a model before the war and had studied at Oxford. No way would she join the Land Army.

Gus had met her a third time, in an Algiers bar that had turned out to be a brothel. Music had been playing, and the other pilots had been rowdy, leering at the women. But Gus's attention had been caught by just one woman, sitting on a tall stool at the end of the bar — an attractive woman who, apart from her dark auburn hair, had been the image of Eunice Hesketh. It had turned out that it was her, though she called herself Clarice Delacroix. She was working for Peacock.

Eventually, Gus finished his letter to Sir Alex. He had accepted the posting to join 161 Squadron and the Special Operations Executive. He put it into an envelope, which he addressed to Sir Alex at 64 Baker Street, London. He'd get one of the servants to post it tomorrow.

CHAPTER 2

Christmas was a pleasant diversion for everyone, but it soon passed. Having enjoyed a quiet time in Winchester with his cousin and aunt, on Boxing Day Flying Officer Staś Rosen had to leave in order to get back to his squadron.

"I think I'll take the train to London with you, Staś, if that's all right?" said Gus. He was taking a chance that Eunice had made it back to England, for he wanted to see her again.

"Of course, I'll be glad of the company. Ready to leave straight after lunch?"

"Perfect," said Gus.

He sped to his room and threw together enough clothes and items of uniform to last a few days.

After lunch, the cousins bade farewell to a tearful Magda and made their way to Winchester station.

"Your mother isn't too well, is she?" said Staś.

"No," said Gus, "she's losing her memory, sadly, and she's so frail these days. I'm worried she'll take a tumble and — well, you know what it's like."

"Yes. I can imagine," said Staś, sympathetically.

That was the end of their conversation, and the journey to London was largely spent looking out of the carriage windows at the frozen Hampshire and Surrey landscape. Bidding farewell to Staś at Waterloo station, Gus travelled to West Hampstead and sought out the small flat that Eunice's father had bought for her. He rang the bell. Soon footsteps could be heard coming down the stairs and the front door opened.

"Bloody hell, if it isn't Gus Beaumont!" Eunice exclaimed. "Come on in. You must be freezing."

"I've brought a bottle of champagne," he said. "Purloined from the mess at Ta Kali. I had supplied them in the first place, after all."

"Lovely," she said. "I'll find a couple of glasses." She walked into the kitchen. "Sit down, Gus, but don't take your coat off. I've only just got back. It'll warm up in here soon."

"How did the journey from Algiers go?" he asked, when Eunice came in with two champagne flutes.

"Not too bad, thanks. Only a two-and-a-half-hour flight from Maison Blanche to Gibraltar. It was fine. This burly old flight sergeant told us there wasn't much grub on board and hoped we'd all eaten. He also said that if we felt sick, there were some paper bags. Are you going to open that?" She was eyeing the champagne bottle.

"Yes," he said, prising out the cork with his thumbs. It shot into the air and Gus poured. "Who else was on the flight?"

"There were three others…" She frowned. "I've become so suspicious of everyone. I'm so bloody tired of all this undercover work."

"You don't have to do it. Just tell Peacock you've had enough."

"No, Gus, I have to see it through. Where was I?" she said, pausing for a sip of champagne. "Oh, yes, there was a woman on my left. Probably an agent, like me. There was no point trying to engage in conversation — we couldn't talk about our work. Anyway, we most likely had nothing else in common. The other two passengers were men, both in uniform. Seated next to me was a naval officer dressed in a tropical white uniform with lots of gold braid on the sleeves, while further away was a Free French soldier, a full lieutenant. I asked the naval officer if we could possibly swap seats. I wanted to be closer to the door. He didn't mind. He stood and I shuffled along, sandwiched between the two men."

"Small aeroplane?"

"Yes, a Lockheed Hudson. There were no seatbelts, but I noticed some parachutes in a rack above us. I wondered whether they were for the crew or passengers. The engines fired up and the Hudson began to move along the runway. The pilot yelled to us through the cabin door to prepare for take-off. Then he increased the engine revolutions and we moved off again, gaining speed. Soon we were airborne.

"There were no windows, nothing to see or do. I told myself I must stop thinking, so I tried to strike up a conversation. I asked the French soldier if he spoke English. He didn't, so we spoke in his own tongue. I introduced myself as Joan, and he told me his name was Eugene Leblanc. He was with the Free Forces, of course. I said that I admired him for what he was doing. He thanked me, but insisted it was General de Gaulle that I should admire. He'd been an inspiration to all of the Free French. I said yes, of course. I told him that I couldn't understand why so many French people put up with the Nazis, and his answer surprised me a little."

"What did he say?"

"He said France is a divided nation."

"Well, we all know that. Half the country is occupied by the Germans, the other half ruled by General Pétain."

"No, it's not just that. He went on to explain that there were many right-wing French in the occupied sector who supported the Nazis. Pétain, he said, was a pro-Nazi dictator. He told me he'd made himself Chief of State and has put a death sentence on de Gaulle. Did you know that, Gus?"

"Golly! No, I didn't."

"He said that even Algeria is split. The Algerians themselves are with de Gaulle, but not the *colons* — they're the French settlers. They are for Pétain. He thought it an utter disgrace."

"Did the others have anything to say about all that?"

"Nothing. I kept him talking — it was fascinating. He said that in France some people resist, a few collaborate, but the majority just try to get on with their lives. And the Resistance is split too. Gaullists, socialists, communists. But now de Gaulle has formed the French National Committee, with himself as president. It's an all-encompassing coalition including Free French forces, like his unit, and resistance fighters ranging from conservative Catholics to communists. In occupied France, in Vichy France, it's the same."

"Sounds like a bloody mess to me. Peacock would be interested, though. He's keen to know which resistance movements we can trust and which are…"

"Reds. Yes, I know. I think Peacock must already know the answers, though. I wonder what happened to Duncan?" She was referring to Lieutenant Duncan Farquhar, a friend from Gus's university days.

"You told me you escorted him as far as the Spanish border."

"Yes. Then I passed him onto a Spanish woman. He must be back in Blighty by now, I suppose."

"I'll try to look him up. I'm seeing Peacock tomorrow. Maybe he knows something."

"Why are you seeing the wing commander?"

"It's about my next posting. Anyway, continue telling me about your journey home."

"I spent three days in Gibraltar before boarding a ship bound for England. Convoy HG 76. It sailed in mid-December. I remember looking out to sea on the second morning and watching two fighter aircraft from the escort carrier — it was HMS *Audacity*. They took off and shot down a Focke-Wulf Condor reconnaissance aircraft."

"Those convoys are bloody dangerous," said Gus.

"*Audacity* was a peculiar ship — it looked like a floating flight deck. But it was comforting to have her with us. Her fighters were kept busy attacking German U-boats during the voyage. Sadly, she copped it just west of Cape Finisterre."

"What happened?"

"Well, I heard a commotion and rushed up on deck to see what it was. There was a fire on the carrier and then an almighty explosion. The naval officer from the Hudson was there. He had his binoculars. I asked him what it was. He said a torpedo must have hit the aviation fuel. One of the merchantmen had fired a snowflake flare. God only knows why. It must have been a mistake. Anyway, it lit the sky and exposed *Audacity*'s silhouette to the German U-boats. Her bow had been blown off and she was sinking. We stood there and watched, mesmerised. The whole scene was illuminated by fire from her own holds. She sank, Gus. She went down quickly, bows first. We could just about see her fighter aircraft, their wings folded, slipping and sliding into those icy Atlantic waters. Oh, those poor, poor men."

They were silent for a moment, and then Gus topped up their glasses. "So tell me, where did you land? London?"

"No. The convoy arrived in Liverpool on the twenty-third of December. I thought about looking up Milly Turner in Salford. But I was too tired. And I needed to be alone. Sorry."

Gus looked at her gaunt face. What had she been through? "Don't worry," he said. "We can catch up with her after this bloody war is over."

"Yes. Anyway, I took a train to London on Christmas Eve. I slept for most of the journey and reached West Hampstead early in the evening. The flat was bitterly cold, Gus. I lit a fire and, once it was going well, I popped to the shops for enough food to tide me over until after Boxing Day. And now you're here." She smiled.

Gus smiled back. "It's nice to see you again."

"Nice to see you, too. But I'm worn out by it all, Gus."

"Just take it easy for a few days, Eunice. You'll soon be back to your old self. I know, why not take a break, a bit of a holiday? Brighton or somewhere."

"Gosh, that's the first time I've been called by my real name in months. It's the best thing, too. I'm Eunice again, alive and back in England, for the time being at least. Yes, I need a holiday. It will give me the chance to think about normal things. About you, Gus. You and me."

At that moment, with Eunice smiling through her exhaustion, Gus realised that he loved this woman. And there was a chance that she loved him too.

Then Bunty burst into his mind. If Eunice returned his feelings, he would have to choose between the two women. Bubbly and fun-to-be-with Bunty, or mysterious and unreliable Eunice, with whom he was in love.

CHAPTER 3

Gus yawned as he emerged from Eunice's flat the following morning, his breath condensing in the cold air. He pulled the collar of his greatcoat up around his neck then set off at a brisk walk towards Finchley Road station. Half an hour later, he was trying not to slip on the icy steps to number 64 Baker Street, the headquarters of the Special Operations Executive, where Wing Commander Peacock was based.

"Congratulations once again on your promotion, Gustaw," said Peacock as he ushered him into his office. "Well deserved, young man."

"I'm guessing it was all your doing?" replied Gus, grateful for the warmth of the small coal-fire in the office.

"I had a small hand in it," Peacock admitted. "Can't have you strutting around our new Special Duties squadron as a mere flying officer now, can we? I'm pleased you decided to accept, by the way. You're exactly the type we need."

"Well, I'm very much looking forward to taking up the opportunity, Sir Alex."

"Good. I'm sure you'll do well. By the way, Squadron Leader Grindlethorpe contacted me. He suggested I have you posted to Burma, or somewhere similarly nasty."

"Did he? I wonder where he is now?"

"As a matter of fact, he's the one working in a hothouse, somewhere in the Western Desert."

Peacock chuckled. It was the first time Gus had ever seen the wing commander relax or show any emotion. Gus joined in with his laughter at Titus Grindlethorpe's misfortune.

"He hates the bloody heat," Sir Alex continued. "So I've had him posted to command a reconnaissance squadron that's supporting the 7th Armoured Division in the North African desert. I can imagine him now, swatting flies from his sweat-covered face. But it won't be for long," said Peacock, sobering. "I want to bring him back."

"Why?"

"To keep an eye on him. And to make use of him. He might be a fuddy-duddy, and he clearly doesn't like you, Gustaw. But Titus does have his merits. He's a damned fine organiser and I think we could use his talents here, in the SOE. We have to liaise more closely with Combined Ops, and I think he may be just the sort we need. I'd like you here as well, but only for a few weeks before you go to clock up your Lysander training. The two of you will just have to tolerate each other."

"Yes, sir." Gus knew there was little point in arguing.

"Anyway, what can I help you with?"

"I need a bit of help, actually, sir. I'm searching for a friend, Duncan Farquhar. Pongo officer. He was in my year at Oxford and I bumped into him again in Calais, just before Dunkirk. He was taken prisoner by the Germans but escaped and — I think — made it home. I'm trying to trace him. Do you know anything?"

"Yes, as a matter of fact I do."

"Do you know where I can find him?"

"He's in London." Peacock looked in a notebook, found what he was looking for, scribbled down an address on a piece of paper and handed it to Gus. "He's staying in town, I believe, but you'd better be quick. He's about to start in Special Ops, too. He'll begin training in the New Year."

So Peacock had recruited Duncan into the SOE as well. Gus wondered why, but there was no point in asking Peacock.

"Thank you," he said, looking at the address. It was in Maida Vale — not too far. "I'll go there now and see if he's in."

CHAPTER 4

Gus walked from Baker Street to the address in Maida Vale that Peacock had given him. He knocked on the door of a large townhouse that had been converted into flats. Duncan opened the door.

"Gus Beamont! Well, well, well, what a surprise! Good to see you, old boy!" Duncan said.

"You too, and congratulations," said Gus, nodding at the three pips on Duncan's epaulettes.

"Thanks. I feel something of a cheat, actually."

"What, for escaping from Germany? I'd say you earned it."

"Do you know what? I was simply bloody lucky."

"Tell me."

"Shall I make a pot of tea?"

"How about something stronger, Duncan? There must be a decent pub around here."

"Good idea. The Black Swan is good. Let's go!"

Ten minutes later they were sitting at a quiet table in the corner of the Black Swan, nursing pints of ale.

"So, you think you were lucky?" said Gus.

"Absolutely. First, I was lucky not to be spotted when I jumped from that moving German POW railway cart. Second, I was lucky when I coshed that German soldier that no blood splattered onto the chap's uniform before I put it on. I hadn't planned it or anything. It was serendipity."

"We all need a bit of luck."

"I was lucky again to have been taken in by a sympathetic French farming family and handed over to the Resistance. It might all have ended terribly."

"You sure it was just luck?"

"Well, I'd taken the trouble to make myself as sure as I could be that those French farmers weren't collaborators. The woman had spat when a lorry load of Jerry soldiers passed by. She was no German lover, that was for sure."

"Well then, you do deserve some credit. Tell me, how did you get out of France?"

"It was via the O'Leary route — an escape line helping Allied servicemen evade capture in Nazi-occupied France and return home to Blighty. To be honest, Gus, I didn't take much notice of what was going on — first because I'd been so damned infatuated with the young woman they gave the job of getting me out…"

Gus frowned — he'd already heard the full story from Eunice — but Duncan didn't notice.

"…and second because I became really unwell with an infection when we reached Lyon. I can't remember much about that period. The woman took care of everything."

"Tell me about her, Duncan."

"She was a French woman called Clarice. Actually, I'm not sure she was French. I've still got a sneaking feeling that she might be English. Her accent was so perfect. She knew Oxford University…"

Gus searched in his wallet for a picture of Eunice, which he showed to Duncan. "Is this her?"

Duncan peered at the photograph. "Yes, it is. So you know her? She's a friend of yours?"

"She's English — she went to Oxford too. I'm a bit surprised you didn't recognise her, to be honest."

"I'd have certainly remembered her had I spotted her before. What's her name?"

"Duncan, I'm not sure I should tell you that. You've been speaking to Wing Commander Sir Alex Peacock, haven't you?"

"Well, I…"

"Come on, I know all about it. He's recruited you for Special Operations. He recruited her as well, and you might go into action together. Better you don't know her real identity."

"She knows mine."

"Well, that's true," said Gus, "but I'd rather not…"

"I understand. But how do you know all this?"

"Peacock knew my parents and he got in touch with me before the war. Let's just say I've helped him out with a few jobs in the past."

"What do you make of him?"

"He's organised and well-connected in the military and government. He is devoted to the country and totally committed to the war."

"Aren't we all?" said Duncan.

"Yes, but it means Peacock's liable to ask us to do some dangerous things."

"War is dangerous, Gus. That's just how it is. But I'd still rather be fighting than sitting it out in a POW camp, even if that means taking risks."

"I thought you'd say that, but I just wanted to warn you. As a friend."

"Thanks. So who's the woman in the picture? Come on, you can tell me."

"Her name's Eunice. Eunice Hesketh."

"Is she your sweetheart, Gus?"

"I don't know… Look, I don't really want to talk about it. It's complicated. Come on, Duncan, let's have another drink and you can tell me all about your adventures. That's what I want to know. Tell me every detail."

Duncan returned from the bar with two more pints of ale. "You know I was captured at Calais?"

"Yes, Eunice told me that."

"May 1940. Seems a lifetime ago. You landed and delivered some spare bits and bobs — I can't remember exactly what they were. But I certainly remember that day; it was just before Dunkirk. When you left, I watched as you taxied to the end of the strip and increase the revs — what a roar! I wished to God I had been in there with you, Gus, and on my way back to England. Then I saw the German fighter appear and line itself up on you. I thought you'd bought it, Gus. How did you get back?"

"Well, that's another tale. Right now I want to know what happened to you."

"After you'd gone, a motorcycle dispatch rider arrived and handed me some papers. I read them, dismissed the rider, then summoned my NCO, Bombardier Albert Cooper. He was a bit surly, I suppose, but he was a good soldier. He died later that day."

"I'm sorry."

"I told Cooper that our orders were to stand and fight. He was rather sanguine about it. I asked him if he had any ideas. He said we might try to dazzle the Germans with our searchlights."

"He had a sense of humour, then?"

"Yes. Motorcycles armed with machine guns came first. Cooper put a shell from the Boys anti-tank rifle into the first one and by the time he opened up on the second, they'd turned around and were off. Next to arrive were armoured cars fitted out with heavy machine guns. They opened fire on us, but didn't do much damage at that range. Cooper put an anti-tank shell into one of the cars, which instantly blew up. Almost as soon as he did, the Germans began landing mortar shells around his emplacement and forced Cooper and the Boys crew to pull out. Shortly afterwards the tanks arrived — Panzer Mark IIIs, five of them. I ordered my men on the Bofors guns to open fire on the German tanks. The lads scored hits, but they couldn't do much damage — they were using time-fused high-explosive shells, you see. They were just bouncing off the German tanks then exploding harmlessly."

"No use at all against German armour," said Gus.

"No. And the bloody Jerries knew it. They knew their tanks were pretty much invincible against light anti-aircraft fire and we had nothing but the Boys rifle that could pierce their armour. They, on the other hand, were putting their guns to good use. They were beginning to get the range of ours. Fire, smoke and explosions filled the air. I realised then that the situation was desperate. A shell exploded behind me, the gun and crew blown to smithereens. I felt an excruciating pain in my left shoulder — shrapnel, I assumed — and saw the body of Bombardier Cooper lying on the ground. It was hopeless. I ordered the men to put down their weapons and surrender."

"That must have been hard."

"It was pointless carrying on. They'd all have died holding up the German tanks and amour for five more minutes. What was the point of that?"

"You did the right thing."

"We were ordered to march back towards the advancing Germans. They treated us pretty well on the whole. Eventually I was taken by train to Germany with a bunch of other POWs — Brits, Czechs, Dutch, all sorts. We were imprisoned at Oflag IX-A/H, near Spangenberg, Northern Germany. Later that same year, in the winter, I was in the process of being moved from Spangenberg to God knows where — somewhere in German-occupied Poland, the CO had been told. That was way too far from Blighty for me, so I jumped from the train."

"That was brave of you, Duncan."

"Some might say foolhardy. It worked, but I knew I was a sitting duck in my British army uniform. So I kept my head down during the day and moved at night. The Germans would think I'd go west, towards Britain — that's where they'd search for me. So I headed east."

"Clever," said Gus. "You kept a cool head."

"I needed to change my clothes if I was going to make it, so I had a think and came up with a plan. The German soldier was smoking. Perfect. I'd studied his movements, a sole sentry at a quiet spot. I found a hefty piece of wood. A fencepost or something. I hit him bloody hard, Gus. A crushing blow, it was. He had no chance. I feel bad about it now, attacking a man from behind, you know?"

"I can see that, yes. It must have been awful. But you had to do it, Duncan."

"God, it was dreadful. He fell forwards and hit the snow-covered ground at that first blow. I pulled the body into some bushes and stripped it of all but underclothes. Then I changed into the German's uniform. It was bloody freezing. It fitted me well enough, though the boots were a bit tight. Then I placed my clothes and the greatcoat over the body and doused it all with the petrol I'd previously stolen. I looked at the man's papers — he was Soldat Daniel Hoffmann. His photograph was a faded mugshot that, with a bit of dirt on my own face, might resemble me. I didn't intend to confront many police or military guards, but if I did, I knew my German was good enough pass me off as a surly, non-conversational German conscript. One of the benefits of a good public-school education, don't you know?"

"Indeed."

"Once I was ready to make my getaway, I set the corpse alight with the dead man's own matches — that's why I'd chosen a smoker."

"Bloody hell, Duncan, and you think your escape was simply good luck. Nonsense, man. And where did all this happen?"

"A small place called Waldkappel. I'd guess it was about twenty miles east of the Spangenberg POW camp. Now that I'd assumed the soldier's identity, I could risk travelling in daylight, but I avoided it when I could. I changed direction, navigating by the moon and stars, and avoiding any large towns. It was freezing cold, though.

"I went south towards Meiningen. From there I headed west towards Frankfurt, walking mostly in the half-light or at night and resting by day. That way I proceeded west towards Saarbrücken. My first big problem was how to cross the bridge over the Saar river at Saarbrücken and into France. There were bound to be guards — police, soldiers, or both. So I found a hidey-hole in the entrance to a storm drain and waited, praying that it wouldn't rain heavily."

"How did you get across the bridge?" asked Gus.

"I remember waking from a fitful sleep at around seven in the evening. There was some movement on the bridge. Lots of off-duty German soldiers heading east across the bridge. It dawned on me that it must be very close to Christmas. Of course, the Germans preferred spending their money on beer and sausages on the German side of the river. I studied the action. Lots of movement eastward up until eight o'clock, then, between ten o'clock and midnight, there was an unsteady stream of drunken soldiers returning to their barracks on the French side of the bridge. It would be fairly easy to feign a degree of drunkenness and tag onto the back of one of these swaying trains of soldiers. It would mean ditching the rifle I took from the German sentry, though. None of the revellers went out armed. So, the next night, I left the rifle in the storm drain and staggered over the bridge with the others. It was easy."

"It doesn't sound easy, Duncan. It sounds damned dangerous!"

Duncan nodded and continued. "Once in France, I needed to take more chances. I couldn't trust the police — this part of France was occupied. I took refuge in a deserted barn with a view over a road junction, and I looked out and surveyed the activity. I saw two young women, busy with farm work. They put out animal fodder and fed chickens. When a lorryload of German soldiers went by and shouted to them, the women turned away. One of them spat on the ground. Not German-lovers, then, I thought. They would have to do. I'd take a chance and put my trust in them.

"So, when the lorry was safely out of sight, I ventured out of the barn and called to the women. My German is good, Gus, and I'm better than passible at both Latin and Ancient Greek. But French? Hardly a bloody word!"

"That's where your schooling let you down," said Gus with a grin.

"I decided that English, even if they didn't understand it, was my safest bet in the circumstances. 'I say!' I shouted to them, waving both arms to show I wasn't armed. 'Don't be fooled by this uniform. I'm English — an English army officer!' They were frightened, but at least they didn't run away.

"One of the women turned to check the road. It was empty. She turned back to me. 'Yes. English. I need help. Clothes,' I said, pointing to the uniform. 'And food.' I put my hand to my mouth, mimicking eating. Amazingly, one of the women spoke a bit of English. 'Yes, yes, come with me,' she said, beckoning me towards the farmhouse building. So, as I say, bloody lucky!"

"I'd say the brave make their own luck, Duncan. So, what happened then? Did the Resistance show up?"

"Yes. First a French chap came on his own, and then he returned the day after with Eunice."

Gus emptied the last of his beer. "Fancy another?"

"Why not?"

Gus went to the bar and came back with two more pints of ale. He sat down, pushing one of the drinks toward Duncan.

"Now," said Gus, "I want you to tell me exactly how Sir Alex recruited you into the SOE."

"Once I was back in Blighty, I was debriefed about the whole thing. It took a couple of days. I thought I was finished, but then I received a letter from Wing Commander Peacock. He summoned me to his office in Baker Street."

"Number sixty-four."

"That's it. I went along and met him there. 'So good of you to come,' he said, as though I had any say in the matter."

"That's him."

"He told me to sit down and tell him about the French. I said they treated me very well indeed. Then he surprised me. He said that wasn't quite what he meant. He wanted to know how they performed, whether the Resistance was fit for purpose. He asked if they were well organised and strategic. Most importantly, he wanted to know whether we could trust them."

"What did you say?"

"Well, I didn't have a bloody clue, so I told him I thought every outfit has room for improvement. He agreed and told me he thought I might be the man to improve them. I told him I had no idea what he meant."

"He wants you to go back to France, I expect."

"Yes. He said that, if I think I can stomach it, I'm to be trained up to go back to France and make contact with some key individuals over there. He wants me to get to know them — find out which of them we can trust and which we can't, then report back to him. He said he was thinking of after the war and asked me if I understood. Well, I took a sip of the tea that Peacock had offered me to stall a bit. Frankly, Gus, I had no idea what on earth the old beggar was on about."

"He wants you to find out which Resistance cells are Reds. You see, after the war — assuming we win it, of course — the government doesn't want any countries flirting with Communism."

"How do you know this?"

"I did a similar job for Peacock in Greece last year. But please, carry on."

"Well, he asked if I could do that for him — 'for king and country' is what he actually said."

"And can you?"

"I told him I would, but explained that I don't speak much French. He said there was no need to worry about that — I'd be put on a crash course to learn enough French to get by — I wouldn't have to convince anyone I actually was French. No, I'd be totally underground and he'd send me with an interpreter — an undercover agent with perfect French. He said he had someone in mind, actually."

Gus stared at Duncan. "He's going to send you in with Eunice, isn't he? Bloody hell."

"I don't know. He didn't give any names. But he said I can start straight after Christmas if I like."

"And you're going to do it?"

"Yes. Peacock said I'm one of very few officers to have escaped from Germany and make it out of occupied France with the help of the Resistance. I'll be a valuable asset to operations in France. So valuable, in fact, that he had me promoted to captain. Another beer?" Duncan asked, noticing that Gus was nursing an empty glass.

"No, thanks. I've got to rush, sorry."

"Shame. But I've had a thought. Fancy a game of rugger at the weekend?"

Gus raised an eyebrow. "Are you serious?"

"Absolutely. I'm putting together a mixed army and air force team to play against a navy XV. We're a bit short in the three-quarters. You played centre for your college, didn't you?"

"Only the 2nd XV."

"Come on, Gus. A run out will do you good. What do you say?"

"I suppose so, as long as you buy the beers afterwards."

"Done!"

CHAPTER 5

Gus had managed to scrounge some rugby boots and shorts. Duncan supplied matching red shirts to the mixed team of army and RAF officers who were assembled in the cramped changing room near the pitch at Repton Avenue in Sudbury.

Duncan had a piece of paper in his hand, with a list of names against positions.

"Bit of a scratch side," he said, "but we'll do what we can. I'm playing full-back and will be captain. Gus, you take inside centre, please."

"All right," he agreed.

"You'll have Archie here at fly-half and Peter outside you," said Duncan, waving towards two army officers. Archie Rafferty wore the uniform of the Royal Scots Fusiliers and Peter Grimes the Royal Dragoons.

Gus offered his hand. "Gus Beaumont, but known as Bouncer in the mess."

Peter grasped Gus's hand firmly. "Pleased to meet you," he said.

Huffing, Archie turned his back and walked away.

"Don't bother about him," said Peter. "He's got a thing about flyboys."

Gus turned a puzzled-looking face to him.

"He was at Dunkirk," Peter added.

"And what does that have to do with me, exactly?"

"You know…"

"Right, chaps, let's get out onto the field!" shouted Duncan, curtailing further discussion.

Gus pulled up his socks and followed the team out from the changing room and onto the rugby field.

Duncan shook hands with the referee and the opposition captain, a burly forward wearing a number eight on his blue shirt. He called heads when the ref tossed a silver coin into the air. Duncan lost the call and the Navy elected to kick-off.

Gus stood on the left side of Archie and slightly behind him. The Navy outside-half kicked the ball high into the sky above the forwards and, as it came down, it was caught by a red-shirted player and a maul ensued. The ball came out to the reds' scrum-half, who passed out wide to Archie. He ran towards the opposition, who advanced towards the line of red-shirted players. Drawing the tackling player, Archie passed the ball to Gus only a split second before his navy counterpart was on him. As Gus caught the pass, the Navy player crunched into his midriff, sending the ball flying forwards.

"Knock-on!" called the referee.

"You clumsy bastard," said Archie. "Can't you flyboys catch?"

"Clumsy? That was a hospital pass. Do you want to get me killed?"

"Shut up and lineout over there," said Archie, pointing to the open side of the pitch.

"Bad pass," said Duncan to Gus. "Archie hasn't got his eye in yet. Don't worry."

A little later in the game it happened again. The reds attacked. Archie had the ball and ran towards a gap between two blue defenders, Gus sprinting at his shoulder. The pass was delayed so that the instant the ball touched Gus, the defending player was on him with another crunching tackle, sending him to the ground. He lay there, winded.

"Get up, you bastard!" shouted Archie.

Gus got to his knees. Then, painfully, he rose up to his full height.

At half time the players stood in two circles, one at either end of the pitch. Gus spotted Archie and walked up to him.

Standing face to face with the fusilier, he growled, "What's this all about, Rafferty?"

"All about? It's about you not being able to catch a rugby ball and side-step a tackle."

"You're deliberately delaying the pass to get me hurt."

"Nonsense. It's you being slow, getting there late. Like your lot were at Dunkirk, you cowardly buggers."

"Listen, Rafferty," said Gus, squaring up to the army officer. "I was at Dunkirk, too, as a matter of fact. My flight sergeant was killed when we were shot at by Bf-109s. Later, I was shot down in France by a Bf-110. I was picked up by the *Royal Daffodil*, crammed with weary, defeated and dejected soldiers from the beaches of Dunkirk. After that, I fought in the Battle of Britian, then in Greece and Malta. I've even faced the enemy on the ground, armed with a Lee Enfield rifle. So I'm not having any accusations of cowardice from you, or from anyone else. From now on, you're going to draw your tackler then give a reasonably early pass that gives me a chance of doing something useful, rather than getting me smashed."

"And if I don't, flyboy?"

"Archie, just do as the man asks," ordered Duncan, "otherwise I'll take you off. One more chance, understood?"

"Understood," said Archie. He turned to Gus. "My brother was killed at Dunkirk," Archie explained. "He was with the Dorset regiment, second battalion. Those boys fought bravely in the rearguard, only to be bombed on the bloody beaches. I was there too. We didn't see many of your fighters in the skies protecting us. But's that's no reason to take it out on you. I apologise, Beaumont."

"The RAF pilots were only following orders," said Gus. "I heard afterwards that Air Chief Marshal Dowding fought a hell of a battle to keep his fighters in reserve to repel a German air attack on England."

"Well, having lived through the Battle of Britian, I'd say Stuffy Dowding was right," said Peter.

"I see that. But it doesn't help the thousands of men we lost at Dunkirk, does it?" said Archie.

"Agreed," said Gus, "but if you ask me, it was a failure of tactics by us and the French, aided by a complete collapse of moral fibre on the part of the French commanders."

"Why do you say that?"

"I was picked up by the Navy and came home from Dunkirk on a steamer. I chatted to a French staff officer who'd witnessed it all first-hand. Bloch, he was called. You might recall him, Duncan. History don at Oxford before the war."

"Yes, I do. He's with the French Resistance now," said Duncan.

"I met him in Lyon. He helped smuggle me out of France once I'd escaped from the POW camp."

Archie offered Gus his hand. "Sorry again."

"Accepted," said Gus. "Now let's get on with this rugby match, shall we?"

The next time Archie ran with the ball, he aimed between two defenders, drew them both and flicked a perfectly timed pass to Gus. Gus accelerated onto the ball, swerved past one defender, drew the Navy full-back and passed the ball out to Peter Grimes. In turn, Peter passed to Duncan, who was on the overlap, and he sprinted over the line to touch down.

"That's better, lads," said Duncan to his teammates, then he turned and placed the ball ready for a kick at goal.

Duncan Farquhar's rugby team finished the game with a narrow defeat to the officers of the Royal Navy. At the invitation of Peter Grimes, after the game all of the players went down to the Household Cavalry officers' mess at the Knightsbridge barracks. Duncan raised a toast to the victors. "Gentlemen, please raise your glasses to the officers of the Senior Service, jolly Jack Tars all of them and damned good kickers of the rugby ball."

"To the officers of the Senior Service," echoed his team, and they all downed their various glasses of beer and wine.

"Thank you kindly," shouted the Navy captain, "and more drinks all round on us!"

"What have you been doing since the evacuation?" Gus asked Archie, as they sat with Duncan and Peter at a round table in the mess bar.

"Not enough, to be honest. I was with our second battalion at Dunkirk, and since then we've been on home defence. Our first battalion is in Egypt, and I'm hoping to get a transfer. More action over there, you know?"

"What about you Peter?" asked Duncan. "What has your outfit been up to?"

"Been in the desert most of the time," replied Peter. "At the moment, most of the regiment is out there as reconnaissance for the 1st Armoured Division."

"So why are you here in London?"

Peter looked around and lowered his voice. "I'm posted to Aldershot, as part of a test team working on a new cruiser tank. The boffins are using a remodelled Rolls-Royce Merlin Mark Three engine in a Crusader as the prototype."

"Blimey," said Gus. "That'll belt out some power!"

"Yes. They've removed the supercharger to downgrade the performance a bit and reversed the direction of engine rotation to match tank transmission. Fitted to a Leyland-built Crusader tank, they're estimating it might make fifty miles per hour."

"And they're letting you drive it?"

"I'm in command of a section of test drivers, actually."

"I expect that speed will be some advantage in the field," said Archie.

"I'm not sure," said Peter. "These faster cruiser tanks have to keep their armour light, to keep the weight down. That means it's often too thin to offer any real protection. More importantly, they don't pack a big enough punch in the gunnery department. In my opinion, we need a good all-round tank that's well armoured, with a powerful gun and decent speed. Fast enough, but not necessarily fifty-miles-per-hour fast."

"What about you, Bouncer?" asked Archie. "What was that about you fighting on the ground with a Lee Enfield?"

"Oh, that," replied Gus, self-deprecatingly. "Well, you see, I'd happened to crash-land on a Greek island and was rescued by the Resistance. They were fighting the Italians and I got mixed up with them. Didn't do that much, actually," he lied.

"A Greek island? Which one?"

"Corfu."

"How did you get back?" asked Peter.

"I pinched an Italian dive-bomber and flew it to Crete."

The three soldiers paused their drinking to stare at him. "Are you serious, Gus?" asked Duncan.

"Absolutely!"

CHAPTER 6

Two weeks after the rugby match, Gus was in Peacock's office when there was a knock on the door.

"Come in!" called Peacock.

Gus wasn't surprised when Titus Grindlethorpe walked through the door. He had heard that Grindlethorpe had recently returned from the desert and was enjoying his first week back in London.

"Morning, Sir Alexander, and… Bloody hell, Beaumont!" Grindlethorpe rounded on Peacock. "What on earth is he doing here?"

"Flight Lieutenant Beaumont is here on my orders. I want his opinion on something later."

Grindlethorpe had taken over liaison between the SOE and Combined Ops, and Peacock wanted a rundown on Operation Archery.

"Everyone I've spoken to seems to be convinced that the raid on Måløy was a success," said Peacock. "You've had time to swat up on it. Is that what Mountbatten thinks?"

"The operation is considered a success, Sir Alex. In most aspects, that is."

"Tell me more," demanded Peacock. "I want details — facts and figures. That's why I brought you back from the desert, Titus!"

"The Navy sent over one cruiser, HMS *Kenya*, and four destroyers. None of our vessels were lost. Our naval assault force managed to sink ten German vessels — some as they were being scuttled to prevent capture."

"Good, good. Any damage to our ships?"

"A little. We anticipated more damage, but there was just one hit — on HMS *Kenya*, Sir Alex. Combined Ops supposes that technical difficulties may have prevented the German coastal artillery from being fully effective. However, the Navy suffered four men killed and four wounded."

"The German army?"

"Our commandos report at least a hundred and twenty Germans killed, and they returned with about a hundred prisoners. They also captured a complete copy of the German Naval Codes. The land operations were carried out in the extreme confusion of close hand-to-hand fighting, with a lot of smoke. This tested the commandos' communication system to the hilt, as you might imagine. As the battle progressed, many messages could only be passed on by word of mouth. Combined Ops know they need to improve on this. The whole operation saw seventeen men killed and fifty-three wounded."

"Seventy casualties? That's more than expected, isn't it?"

"I believe so. German opposition in the town was much stiffer than was anticipated."

"Were the Jerries expecting us, Titus?"

"No, we don't think so. But our men did encounter a Gebirgsjäger unit in the area."

"Gebirgsjäger?"

"Mountain troops, Sir Alex. Experienced men. Most unfortunate."

"And they account for the losses?"

"Yes. They turned out to be a unit of crack troops from the Eastern Front. They were on leave. Their proficiency in sniping and street fighting caused the operation to develop into a bitter house-to-house battle. Apparently one of them was still sniping at our men when the last of the commandos were re-embarking."

"Are you sure they were on leave? They weren't tipped off?"

"Absolutely sure. Just damned bad luck."

"So, Titus, why didn't we know they were there?"

"That's what Combined Ops would like to know. They blame you, sir. At least, they are blaming the SOE."

"And what do you think?"

"Not enough reliable Norwegian spies, I suppose. By the way, the commander of the Norwegian Independent Company that fought beside our commandos was unfortunately killed in an attack on the German headquarters."

"That's a pity."

"Well, it might fire up the Norwegians' spirits. By the way, over seventy loyal Norwegians were brought back. And several Quislings."

"What about the RAF? How did we do?"

"The RAF provided air cover for more than seven hours and undertook diversionary raids elsewhere. To obscure the path of the advancing troops as they landed on the beaches, smokescreens were provided by bombs from a number of Hampdens."

"I suppose Butch Harris objected."

"I'm sure he would have, but the Air Marshal was actually in the USA at the time. He was attending the Arcadia Conference in Washington DC. Anyway, the smoke worked very well, by all accounts. Throughout these procedures, air cover was provided by Beaufighters and Blenheims from Wick and Shetland. However — and this isn't good news, Sir Alex — eleven of our aircraft were shot down."

"Eleven?"

"Yes. Two Hampdens and two Beaufighters were lost. Which is poor, but we also lost seven Blenheims."

"Those Blenheims are bloody useless as heavy fighters," growled Peacock.

"They're not much better as light bombers," Gus chipped in. "I've flown them."

"We also had thirty-one airmen killed," continued Grindlethorpe.

"Bugger! And Dickie? What does Dickie think of it?"

"Oh, Mountbatten thinks it a great success. He's taking all the glory, of course."

"Of course! And blaming us for lack of intelligence on those bloody mountain troops. But he didn't even command Combined Ops then."

"Quite," said Grindlethorpe, "but a little thing like that won't stop Mountbatten claiming the credit. He's now saying it proves conclusively the complete interdependence of all three arms of the military in modern warfare."

"I think he's probably right, there," said Peacock.

"And he's gunning for a much larger operation next. He wants to see if we can capture a port."

"Really? A port? Where, Titus?"

"Oh, goodness me, I don't know that."

"But where do you think, Titus? If I twisted your arm and forced you to say, where would you plumb for?"

"Well, I'd say somewhere on the Channel coast rather than the North Sea. France, not Belgium. Calais and Boulogne are closest, but probably too obvious. Anywhere west of Fécamp is too far away, except Cherbourg, of course."

"Cherbourg, then? Or Le Havre, perhaps? Is it too far?"

"Le Havre's too far, I think. Cherbourg? Well, it's all alone on its little peninsular, but…"

"Come on, man, I've not fetched you all the way from the desert for wishy-washiness! Where? Gustaw, what's your opinion?"

Gus studied the map on Peacock's desk. "If pushed, I'd go for Dieppe. It certainly looks favourable."

"Yes, it'll be Dieppe, I should think," Grindlethorpe agreed, not to be outdone.

"When?"

"Summer, we can suppose," said Gus. "Any raid will need calm seas, and, assuming a night-time voyage and dawn attack, a high tide in the early morning is most desirable."

"I agree," said Peacock, placing his mug of tea on the map and taking a closer look at it. He took a ruler and measured the distance from Dieppe to the nearest British port, Newhaven.

"Sixty-six nautical miles," he said. "Certainly close enough. If a small force could sail from Scapa Flow to Norway, a larger one could easily get from Newhaven or Portsmouth to Dieppe. But there must be no mistakes. No stumbling upon experienced German mountain troops on leave, eh, Titus?"

"No. No mistakes, Sir Alex."

"Combined Ops needs intelligence," said Peacock. "A survey of the beach and a report on the German defences at least. There are sure to be French Resistance cells in the area. But no SOE presence there. None of our agents there. I want you to get on to that, Titus. See to it, understood?"

"Understood, Sir Alex."

CHAPTER 7

Gus walked towards Soho. He ignored the bars and pubs; instead, he strolled along Greek Street, then took the side road, looking for the tearoom where he usually met Eunice. There it was, still standing; it had survived the Luftwaffe's best efforts. He went in. There were plenty of free tables so Gus sat at one by a window, so that he might see Eunice arrive. American big band music was playing. A couple moved around the polished dancefloor.

In the event, Eunice took him by surprise. She arrived from the opposite direction to that which he'd expected and walked into the place without him seeing her.

"Hey, mister, want to dance?" she asked.

"Maybe later," he said, smiling. "Tea and scones?"

"Yes, please."

"Nice shoes," he commented.

"Oh, these? Paid a bloody fortune for them at Selfridges. I needed a new pair of shoes when I got back from —" she lowered her voice to a whisper — "France. Glad you like them. I wanted something smart but practical."

Gus looked at her shoes, a pair of lace-up brogues with a one-inch heel. They looked comfortable, yet stylish.

"The shop assistant strongly recommended the black. She said they'd go with anything. But I told her I'd take the brown ones."

"Any particular reason for that?"

"The old French ones I had were black and badly worn. I have been wearing them for months on end. If I'm sent back to France, then the SOE can buy me a new pair of French shoes. Do you know, Gus, once I'd bought these, I came straight here, put them on, and threw the damned French things straight into a bin in the ladies' room."

"You came here?"

"Yes. I sat there —" she pointed — "with a pot of tea in front of me. The music came to an end. One of the waitresses changed the disc. Then Glenn Miller's 'Moonlight Serenade' filled the room. How ever did they know that I love that tune, Gus? Then I heard ... well, I thought I heard someone behind me ask, 'Shall we dance?' Slowly I turned around. There was nobody there."

"But you thought it was…?"

Eunice didn't answer. "What about my hair?" she said, changing the subject. "It'll take weeks to grow out. Had I better dye it again?"

Gus looked at Eunice's hair and smiled. He turned to the dancefloor. Just one couple were there: a sergeant in army uniform and a young woman in the Women's Auxiliary Air Force uniform. As they danced a foxtrot, Gus saw tears appear in Eunice's eyes.

"Would you like to dance, Eunice?"

"Yes, please."

They joined in with the foxtrot, then danced a quickstep followed by a waltz.

"Tea's getting cold," said Eunice. "Let's have a breather."

They sat down and she continued her story. "Two days after my last visit here, I was bound for Brighton. I'd found a little bed and breakfast in the small ads of one of last summer's newspapers. I'd rung Mrs Jennings, the landlady, the previous day. I'd told her I needed a single room, just for a few days. She told me they weren't generally open in the low season. I said I was really desperate. I lied that I just had to get out of

London for a short while because my fiancé had been killed in a bombing raid. Horrible of me, wasn't it?"

"No."

"Mrs Jennings said she supposed she could get a room together, for a small consideration. I told her I'd pay half as much again as her usual rates, cash on arrival. She agreed and asked when she should expect me."

"And what's Brighton like at this time of year? Quiet, I expect."

"Quiet, yes. And cold. I walked a lot. I remember one day walking slowly into that bitter, easterly wind. I pulled my scarf up around my ears. To the left there was an uneven line of green-brown kelp and darker, reddish, dulse. To my right I could hear the sea, gently swishing up the shingle and then retreating more noisily. It's all shingle there, you know? Not sand. I looked behind me as I walked. There was no trail. No imprints. And that set me thinking. I hadn't been there, had I?"

"What on earth do you mean?"

"I looked out to sea, towards France. Occupied France. Vichy France. What did it matter? What difference was there? I've lived in both. Lived, worked, and fought in both. Or, to be precise, Clarice has. Eunice hasn't set foot out of Britain since the start of the war. I looked behind me again. It was as though I hadn't trodden on that shore at all. And I hadn't, had I? I mean, Eunice Hesketh had. Yes. But Clarice Delacroix hadn't."

Gus stared at her, perplexed.

"Don't you see, Gus? I didn't know who I was. And I still don't. Am I Clarice the undercover agent? Or am I Eunice, with my desk job that I can't talk to anyone about? Hush-hush, careless talk costs lives, and all that. A live-in job, from which I very rarely get away to keep in touch with friends. They've all given up on me, except you. On that beach, in that moment, I thought I was going mad. Am I, Gus? Am I losing my mind?"

"No, you're not going mad, Eunice. You're tired and stressed. Who wouldn't be?"

"Then the rain turned to sleet and the sleet thickened, turning to snow. I'd never been by the sea during a snowfall. Over to my left, beyond the line of seaweed, the snow settled, turning the ground white. I turned away from the wind and looked out over that grey, uninviting sea. Somewhere, far beyond the horizon was France. Will Peacock send me back, Gus?"

"I don't know."

"I'm not sure I can do it again."

"You don't have to."

"I had a bathroom to myself at Mrs Jennings' boarding house. There were no other guests. I put a flannel around the brass plug, wedged it firmly into the plughole and turned on the hot tap. Back in my room, I undressed, wrapped a fluffy, pink towel around myself, and picked up the bath salts I'd bought earlier and an old, dog-eared copy of Victor Hugo's *The Last Day of a Condemned Man.* I'm telling you all this, Gus, because it seems to help me."

"It's all right, Eunice. We have time for the details."

"I sprinkled salts into the steaming tub and immersed myself in the hot water. I closed my eyes and relaxed, and after ten minutes I picked up my book. I'd begun reading it on the train down from London. I enjoyed the story. Do you know it?"

"No."

"It's all about a man vilified by society for a crime and condemned to death. He wakes every morning knowing that this day might be his last, which reminded me of the brave RAF pilots like you, Tunio and Staś. Anyway, as the hours pass, the man knows that he is powerless to change his fate, which reminded me of myself, Gus. I'm powerless. Can I keep up the pretence any longer? Or can I get out, tell Peacock I've had enough?"

"Yes, you could do that, Eunice."

"Oh, Gus. What the bloody hell should I do?"

CHAPTER 8

A few days after his meeting with Eunice, Gus was making his way to Peacock's office upon the wing commander's summons. He spotted Squadron Leader Piotr Krawiec on Baker Street, apparently heading the same way. Gus hadn't seen Krawiec since before the war, when he and Peacock had sent Gus across Germany and into Poland with a message for Captain Tunio Nowacki.

"*Dzień dobry*, Beaumont," said the tall Pole. "Fancy bumping into you."

"Likewise, sir."

"I was sorry to hear about your father's death."

Gus nodded.

"Do give Mrs Beaumont my sincere best wishes when you see her next."

"Thank you, I shall."

"I see you've been promoted. Congratulations, flight lieutenant."

"Thank you, sir."

Climbing the few steps up to the front door of the SOE headquarters, Krawiec seized the heavy door knocker and banged it loudly. An instant later the door was opened by a corporal.

"Good morning, sir."

"Are you new here?" asked Krawiec.

"Yes, sir."

"I'm here to see Wing Commander Peacock."

"Yes, sir. One moment." The soldier looked down his sheet. "Your name please, sir?"

"Squadron Leader Krawiec."

"Ah, yés, sir. That way please." He pointed towards the staircase. "The door on the left, off the first landing."

"Yes, I know," said Krawiec as he climbed the stairs, Gus following closely behind. They walked into Peacock's office to find that Grindlethorpe was already there.

"Ah, Piotr. So nice to see you," said Peacock. "Do take a seat."

"Likewise, Sir Alex," said the Pole as he sat down.

"You haven't met Squadron Leader Grindlethorpe before. He's new here."

"Grindlethorpe," said Krawiec, nodding.

"And young Beaumont is here between postings — he's helping with some admin. Anyway, I understand you have news for me, Piotr?"

"News, yes. And a request."

"Let's begin with the news, shall we? Is it good news or bad news? Oh, Gustaw, please could you go and organise a pot of tea for the three of us?"

"Yes, sir," said Gus, leaving the room. When he returned, he paused outside the door and listened.

"You know about the Whitley drop?" he heard Krawiec ask.

"No, do tell us," said Peacock.

"A brand-new Whitley bomber carried out a flight to Poland earlier this year. It successfully dropped three agents and supplies. It completed the seventeen-hundred-mile round trip in just under twelve hours."

"Admirable. I'm impressed."

"But the weather and conditions were perfect that night. We don't think the Whitley is suitable. Its service ceiling is too low as well. We need better aircraft, Sir Alex."

"Hmm."

"We found out later that the agents were dropped in the wrong place…"

"Oh dear, that's not good."

"We think it would be preferable in future operations to use all-Polish crews. Apart from anything else, they are more familiar with the country. If they are downed, they'll have a much better chance of getting away."

"And you think you have capacity for that?"

"Yes. I'm confident we can have all-Polish crews operating as part of 138 Squadron at RAF Stradishall. It's just up the road from us, sir."

"I'll see what I can do. What type of aeroplanes would you like, Piotr?"

"We need something fast and long-range, and it must be a bomber so as not to attract attention."

"Wellingtons?"

"No, Liberators."

"Not a bloody hope! Unless the Polish government-in-exile can buy some from the Yanks," Grindlethorpe put in.

"What about Handley Page Halifaxes, then? Give me a couple of those."

"Do you know," said Peacock, before Grindlethorpe could speak again, "that RAF Bomber Command has a regular frontline strength of around four hundred aircraft? Butch Harris doesn't like his kites being used for anything other than dropping bombs on Jerry. Let me think about it."

"I'm afraid it's a little more urgent than that, Sir Alex. The Reds are dropping supplies for the Armia Ludowa," said Krawiec. "Make of that what you will. We see it as bad news."

"Are they, by Jove? The Armia Ludowa? Perhaps you could remind me…"

"The People's Army. Communists. They have never shown loyalty to the Polish government-in-exile or the Polish Home Army. The Russians are aiding them. You know what that means?"

"That Uncle Joe wants to see a Communist Poland after the war. Well, that's hardly a surprise, is it?"

"No, I agree. But this brings it closer. We simply can't let it happen, can we?"

"No, quite. What do you suggest, Piotr?"

"We already support the Polish Home Army, and its leaders show no animosity towards the Armia Ludowa. No point in approaching them. But the NSZ, they hate…"

"Sorry, Piotr. The NSZ?"

"The Narodowe Siły Zbrojne, or the National Armed Forces. They're the third largest underground armed force fighting in Poland. They hate the Reds. They fight the Communists wherever they encounter them. It cuts both ways — no love lost between them, you might say."

"Their politics?"

"Extremely right wing, almost as bad as the Nazis."

"And you think we should support them? Arm them?"

"I do."

"Hmm," muttered Peacock.

"I said there was a request, Sir Alex."

"Go on."

"We already drop supplies, weapons, ammunition and explosives. We want to drop agents. We have a small team ready. They'll link up with the NSZ and organise them to fight the Reds. We'll instruct them to do nothing else — they should even ignore the Germans. They need to eliminate the Armia Ludowa; we can't let a Communist Poland happen."

"You really think that would be a good idea, Piotr?"

"I'm certain."

"How, exactly, would you do this?"

"We would use a Halifax to fly over Poland and drop the team in. But we don't have trained aircrew. We need a favour."

"Your list does go on, Piotr," said Peacock dryly.

"We need a Halifax-trained crew with as many Poles as possible. That young half-Pole, Beaumont — he's a flyer. He has a good record and he's a flight lieutenant now, I see. I'd like him to lead the operation, if possible. Is he available?"

On hearing this, Gus judged that it was time for him to re-enter the room. He knocked on the door and carried in a tray of tea and biscuits.

"Gustaw, Squadron Leader Krawiec would like to borrow you for a job," said Peacock. "What do you think?"

"You're too good a pilot to be an office boy fetching tea, Beaumont. Fancy piloting a Halifax to Poland for me? Parachute drop?" added Krawiec.

"I don't fly heavies, sir," said Gus. "I was a fighter pilot, and now I'm on Special Ops and about to convert to night flights in Lysanders."

"Then you must be a good navigator, yes?"

"Top-notch, sir."

"Exactly what we need, then. Can I borrow you?"

"It's really up to Sir Alex."

"Well, perhaps I could spare him for one mission, I suppose," said Peacock with a frown.

"Sir Alex," piped up Grindlethorpe. "Surely we must do what we can to prevent Poland turning Red?"

"Just for this one mission, I promise," continued Krawiec.

Peacock hesitated, visibly troubled. At last, he said, "Well, I suppose so. If he agrees to do it, of course."

"Of course. All of my men are volunteers."

"Sir Alex," said Grindlethorpe, "we simply can't let a Communist Poland happen!"

"Quite," Peacock conceded. "Yes, Piotr, you can have him, but as I say, just for this one job."

Later, once the details had been thrashed out, Peacock closed the door on Krawiec and Grindlethorpe and returned to his desk.

"If I'm honest, Gustaw, I don't trust those Poles," Peacock confided, keeping his voice low. "To be completely honest, I don't want a Polish section of the SOE. The Poles collapsed against the Nazis in 1939, their forces devastated. Yes, some of their pilots escaped, but only with our help. No doubt there are some fine Polish pilots like Urbanowicz, Zumbach and your cousin, Stanislaw Rosen."

"But you think most of them are unreliable and far too gung-ho, I suppose?" said Gus, bristling a little. His mother was Polish, as were his cousins.

"Yes, frankly I do, and now Krawiec is working on the development of a Polish SOE based at Audley End. And he wants heavy bombers to support it. Nonsense! And why is Grindlethorpe so keen for you to go along as navigator?"

"Probably because he thinks it's a risky mission and he hopes the Halifax, or perhaps just me, won't return."

"Ah," said Peacock, "that will be it."

CHAPTER 9

Gus offered his hand to the young flying officer who stood outside the officers' mess at RAF Tempsford, near Sandy in Bedfordshire. "Flight Lieutenant Gustaw Beaumont, but call me Bouncer. Looks like you're my pilot," he said, in perfect Polish.

"Karol Błaszczykowski," said the officer, eyes on the braid on Gus's sleeve. "You're a bit over-ranked for this, aren't you?"

"Long story. I'll tell you on the return flight."

The mission was called Operation Lodz for no other reason than that it was the next Polish city arranged alphabetically on Piotr Krawiec's list. But this wasn't a supply drop from a Whitley; Peacock had procured a four-engined Halifax.

"Flown these birds before?" asked Gus.

"Of course, twelve sorties," said Karol. "Bombing raids over Germany. Nothing like this."

"Don't worry. Compared with a raid, this will be a breeze. Our course keeps us away from German fighters and flak."

"Talk me through it."

"We'll fly over East Anglia, rising to eighteen thousand feet, towards the northern extremity of the Frisian Islands. From there we'll cross Denmark at height, hook south towards the Polish coast at Koszalin and on to the drop zone near Żarki."

Karol nodded. "Come and meet the rest of the crew," he said, leading Gus to a hut. Inside sat four airmen, who stood and saluted. Karol began to introduce them. "Flying Officer Tomasz Bandrowski is the co-pilot and flight engineer. Flight Sergeant Ciupa is the wireless operator and gunner. The other air-gunners are Flight Sergeants Dubiel and Kałużny. One or other of them will also act as our dispatcher. We don't need a bomb-aimer, obviously."

"Obviously," agreed Gus. "Where are the Joes?"

"Joes?"

"The SOE agents."

"Ah, they over there in the other hut. But I don't think they're agents. They're more like assassins, armed to the teeth. They're being kept separate."

"They need to be briefed about the drop. Come on, we'll do it together."

Gus and Karol strolled over to the solitary hut on the far side of the strip.

"I think they're all Palestinian Jews," said Karol. "I overheard two of them speaking. They began in Polish, but switched to something else."

"Yiddish, maybe?"

"I think it may have been Hebrew."

Gus banged on the door. "Hello?" he shouted in Polish. "May we come in?"

The reply came in the affirmative and Gus walked into the hut. Five men sat around a table. One of them was staring at Gus and he thought he recognised him. Gus wracked his memory. Where had he seen this man before? Yes, that was it — in Palestine earlier this year, when he'd had to report to his old squadron. While in the country, he had taken the opportunity to visit his Uncle Theodore, who had introduced Gus to Jakob and his family.

"Well, well," said Jakob, "the last time we met was in Jerusalem. You threatened my cousin Dawid during a heated exchange. Do you remember me?"

"How could I forget?" Gus thought for a few moments. "It's Joselewicz, isn't it? Jakob Joselewicz."

"Good memory. I see you've been promoted. Congratulations. I'm not surprised. I think you would have knocked Dawid's head off, had I not stopped you." Jakob stood, saluted, and offered Gus his hand.

"You're in British uniform, I see," said Gus.

"British, Polish, what does it matter? I'm a Jew and I'll fight for my people. We all will." He turned to the other grim-faced Jewish fighters.

"We need to brief you about the drop," said Gus.

"Go ahead."

"Karol?"

"We'll fly past the DZ once to check the lights are lit and gauge the wind direction. We'll rise to about one thousand feet, then I'll lose height and turn into the wind to slow the kite down as much as possible. At that point, I'll switch on the red light and one of the flight sergeants will join you. He'll be in RT contact with me."

"I'll try to come back too," said Gus, "just to wish you luck."

"There's no need."

"Well, we'll see."

"On my order, the red light will go green and the dispatcher will shout out the order to jump. He'll push you out of the Joe hole one at a time. We can't have any hesitation."

"I can assure you that none of my men will hesitate, Flying Officer," said Jakob. "How low will you be able to get?"

"The land is flat all around, so I should be able to get low. I won't drop you any higher than four hundred feet — you and your men would be blown all over the place — and I won't drop you at less than two hundred and fifty. You wouldn't

58

survive it. I'll tell the dispatcher our height at the point of the drop, if that helps."

"It helps to know how long we've got," said Jakob, with a smile. "Please get as low as you can. A heavy landing is preferable to German bullets."

At last they were ready for take-off. The Joes, lugging weapons and heavy parachutes, had clambered up ladders into the Halifax, and all of the crew were at their positions, strapped in and ready to go. Karol taxied to the far end of the strip and soon the solitary converted bomber was in the air.

The flight was uneventful. The Joes found it boring. Jakob managed to sleep. Eventually, Gus and one of the NCOs, Flight Sergeant Jozef Dubiel, came into the hold to join them.

"We're almost at the drop zone," said Dubiel, the dispatcher on this sortie.

Jakob roused his men as the red light came on, glowing in the dark of the hold.

"Good luck," said Gus.

Jakob nodded. "Hook up!" he called. "Equipment check!"

The red light went green. "Jump!" Dubiel shouted above the noise.

The men showed no hesitation. One by one they dropped through the Joe hole cut into the bottom of the aircraft. Gus watched as they tumbled out of the Halifax into a dark but clear sky. As they fell, their parachutes opened and the brave men floated down towards occupied Poland. The Halifax soared away, gaining height as it did so, and Gus made his way back to the cockpit.

The converted bomber turned and came in for its second approach. It came over the drop zone and Dubiel pushed out four boxes, each attached to a static line. As the Halifax headed for home, Gus saw four smaller parachutes open. On the ground there would be Polish Resistance fighters to greet the men, help remove the parachutes and gather together the few boxes of supplies that had followed them down.

"Something's wrong!" shouted an agitated Dubiel into the RT as he gazed down from his position over the Joe hole.

"What is it?" asked Gus.

"They've been rumbled! The bloody Germans knew we were coming!" he shouted furiously.

As Karol swung the Halifax around and picked up a course for home, Gus could see flashes on the ground below — small arms. The agents were being shot at.

"We've been betrayed," said Karol.

"We don't know that," replied Gus.

The crew were silent for most of the return flight. Understandably, nobody felt like talking about what had happened.

As they approached the Dutch coast, flak suddenly exploded around them.

"Strap in," ordered Karol over the RT as the heavy aeroplane juddered as the anti-aircraft fire burst around them. Then: "We've been hit!"

"Keep control of her!" shouted Gus.

"Bloody thing feels like it's falling from the sky."

After regaining control, Karol followed his training religiously. "Bouncer," he said, "do a crew check for me, please."

Gus did so and reported back. "Dorsal turret gunner's dead. Everyone else is fine."

"Poor Radosław. Everyone check equipment and instruments," ordered Karol.

All maps and charts were there, all major instruments including their radios were in order, but the compass was down and there were sparks flying from severed wiring in the fuselage.

"Do you know exactly where we are, Bouncer?" asked Karol.

"Yes," said Gus.

"Then we'll shut down all electrics to guard against the risk of fire. Everyone get a parachute ready."

Karol climbed to a higher altitude in order to save fuel. At around eleven thousand feet one of the port engines began to stall. The altimeter couldn't be trusted. Survival was now the only goal.

Gus looked to the sky to locate the constellations that would guide them home. Eventually, he was able to confirm they were over their base.

Karol started the standard distress procedure. He circled the Halifax until the ground crew picked them up on radar and provided homing searchlights. It worked, but as Karol made his approach and reduced the plane's speed, it swung and yawed violently. They had to go round again. This time, Karol approached low and fast, and landed the Halifax safely.

That night, none of the crew could sleep. They stayed together in the mess, Gus included, smoking, drinking and talking.

CHAPTER 10

Two months later, Gus was back at RAF Tempsford, this time attending the basic training for the Special Duties squadron. It usually took about a month for a pilot to complete, but Gus had lots of experience to draw on.

"You've taken to it like a duck to water, Mr Beaumont, sir," said Sergeant Timms, the instructor.

Gus had flown Westland Lysanders at the beginning of the war, when he'd been posted to an army liaison squadron. He knew the aeroplane well and had had hours of flying time in them. He'd even attacked an advance patrol of a German Panzer division in a Lysander in May 1940 — though it hadn't gone quite according to plan, much to Squadron Leader Grindlethorpe's chagrin. Gus also had lots of night-flying experience — not everyone's forte.

Gus brought the Lysander down with only the hint of a bump, much to the relief of Timms. As he parked the Lizzie, he felt down by his left hand for the tail trim wheel, which was beside the throttle. There was no way of countering a badly trimmed tailplane once the Lizzie was powering along a runway. Gus moved the wheel until it was fully forward, ready for take-off.

The other pilots in training were a mixed bunch, but all of them had an above average pilot rating. Recruitment wasn't exactly advertised. Some pilots, like Gus, were drawn into the SOE squadron by personal contacts. Others had been recruited due to their experience in escaping from the Continent. Robert 'Paddy' O'Brian was one such.

"Tell us what happened, Paddy," said one of the flying officers in the mess.

"You really want to know?"

"We do," chorused the men.

"It was a moonlit night and the wild wind blew fiercely over…"

"Just the gist of it will do," said Gus.

"My Wellington was shot down over Belgium on the way home from a raid. Luckily, I was picked up by the Belgian Resistance, passed on to the French and was smuggled down into the Vichy sector. Really good, well-oiled system they've got. Anyway, I was eventually taken to a bit of outback near Tours, and one night a Lizzie turned up and brought me and two others back to RAF Tangmere."

"And you volunteered for this outfit?"

"I was invited, actually. It made sense — I knew the ropes and had night-flying and navigation experience."

Training required the new pilots to be extremely comfortable with the layout of the aircraft's controls. Here, Gus had an advantage, having flown Lizzies before. Nevertheless, he read through the pilot's manual, which included ten pages of handling and flying notes. He sat on a parachute in the cockpit and worked his way around all of the controls until he was sure he could find each and every one of them blindfolded.

The Lysander was a high-winged monoplane designed for close support of the army, and the pilot had excellent views on both sides. The aeroplanes belonging to 161 Squadron had been modified for their new, covert role. The undersides of the aircraft were painted black to help conceal them from searchlights. Gone was the rear gunner's equipment, and the rear cockpit could accommodate three or four Joes. A ladder was fixed to the port side so that the agents could clamber in and out more easily. Finally, a gigantic, torpedo-shaped, one-hundred-and-fifty-gallon petrol tank was slung under the fuselage, giving the Lizzies an enormous range of over one thousand miles.

Many of the pilots on the course had also qualified as navigators. Self-reliance in navigation was an important quality for SOE pilots. Many judged it a more essential skill than piloting the aircraft itself.

Like the others, Gus had to learn how to work out a course to his target and back. The course set was made up of a string of pinpoints, navigational terrain features that were identifiable and whose location was sure. Out on sorties, the pilots flew from pinpoint to pinpoint, staying inside a flak-free corridor, until they reached the target area.

They practised flying by sight alone, first by day over England and then by night. Night navigation had to be done without making use of the radio to ask for a homing bearing. They just flew from navigation point to navigation point. Again, Gus had an advantage. Bunty had talked him through the principle back in 1940; then he'd taken that Defiant over to France for Peacock, telling the rear gunner the compass had broken.

The night flights were repeated time and again. Next they practised night-time landings and take-offs from an area of grassland at a 'dummy' airfield, RAF Somersham, near Tempsford. The rough grass approximated to a typical landing ground in occupied France.

The final test was to take off from RAF Tangmere near Chichester. On a moonlit night, the pilots were to navigate over France, to a target south of Saumur. Although based at RAF Tempsford, 161 Squadron operated out of RAF

Tangmere, as this increased the range and offered a more convenient rendezvous for the pilots and their Joes.

Gus and Paddy O'Brian had flown down from Tempsford to Tangmere, where they had been ordered to report not to the officers' mess, but to a large cottage that stood opposite the main gated entrance to the Tangmere base.

"The SOE Flight is being kept apart from the other squadrons based here," said Paddy. "We don't eat in the mess. They cook here."

"Nothing wrong with that. Genuinely cloak-and-dagger stuff."

It was more a house than a cottage. In fact, it had been converted from a number of seventeenth-century cottages. The walls were thick, the ceilings low and the windows small. Upstairs were five bedrooms, each now packed with as many beds as could be fitted in. Gus and Paddy shared a room.

In the house's ops room, they faced a large map of France that had areas of flak marked in red. One of the senior instructors pointed to an area south of the River Loire.

"Here's the target," said the instructor. "The exact coordinates are in your pack. All you need to do is fly out there, turn round, come back and tell me exactly what you saw down there. We've got full moonlight and good weather tonight and tomorrow. You can decide between yourselves who goes tonight and who waits."

"Toss you for it," said Paddy.

Gus nodded. "Heads I go tonight."

Paddy dug in his pocket and brought out an old penny. He tossed it up into the air and let it fall to the floor. It span briefly, then settled on tails.

"You go tonight, Paddy. Good luck."

They stood in the dark on the grassy runway, looking at the black-painted Lysander. It looked very different to the Lizzie Gus had flown in 1940. It could carry up to three Joes at a time; they could sit on a rear-facing bench that had been installed where the rear gunner and his twin Browning machine-guns might otherwise have sat.

"Good luck, Paddy!" shouted Gus, saluting his friend as he clambered into the cockpit.

He watched as the Lysander took off into the wind, then turned to port, picking up its route to France.

Paddy landed hours later and was whisked away to ensure he didn't spill the beans to anyone.

The following night it was Gus's turn. After eating a top-notch mixed grill supper prepared by Flight Sergeant Bill Booker, one of the two NCO minders who looked after SOE pilots at the cottage, Gus got into the cockpit just as Paddy had done and went through the checks. He started the engine. The ground crew removed the chocks and Gus taxied the Lysander to the leeward end of the strip.

With the brakes fully applied, Gus pushed forward on the throttle lever with his left hand to open up the powerful Bristol Mercury engine. Once it was almost up to maximum prop speed, he let off the brakes and the Lizzie moved along the strip, picking up speed. Once he was at the safety speed of seventy knots, Gus eased back on the stick and climbed away. The Lysander was airborne within yards and heading due west, into wind

Once airborne, he turned to port and picked up his first compass bearing, which took him over the Channel, crossing the French coast at Cabourg. He was aiming for that narrow corridor between Ouistreham and Le Havre that was free of heavy anti-aircraft fire. He climbed to eight hundred feet, well above any light flak. Once past Caen, he altered course and steered towards Saumur.

He saw the moonlit Loire river and the city, checked his compass and altered course slightly to take him over the target. There it was! Gus saw a rectangle of light. He circled it. The lights must be illuminating the fence wire so that guards might spot escapees. It was a good choice by the SOE instructors. The bright lights made it a unique pinpoint. Once he'd returned to base and reported correctly, confirming he'd completed the journey, he would be made operational.

He couldn't wait. Gus turned for home, making for the same flak-free corridor to cross the French coast, then heading for Tangmere.

He clambered out of the cockpit using the Joe ladder and made his way to the squadron leader's office for his debrief.

"It's a prison camp," he said. The squadron leader nodded his approval. Gus was operational.

CHAPTER 11

Paddy O'Brian slammed the morning paper down onto the dining table in the officers' mess.

"Have you seen this? It's disgusting! An RAF serviceman has been convicted of those awful murders in London. You know, the Blackout Killer?"

"Some of the papers called him the Blackout Ripper," said Gus. "He's RAF? Really?"

"Listen to this," said Paddy, and he began reading out loud. *"Gordon Cummins, who was based at the Air Crew Receiving Centre in Regent's Park, was convicted of the murder of a thirty-four-year-old woman, Evelyn Oatley, and sentenced to death."*

"I suppose the blackout gives cover to all sorts of wrongdoing. It's a bad business. Anyway, I've got the weekend off, so less bad news please."

"A weekend off! What a thing! Do you have plans?" asked Paddy.

"I'm going to visit a friend."

"A lady friend?"

"Yes."

"Don't do anything I wouldn't do."

"As a matter of fact, she's an invalid. Wheelchair-bound."

"Sorry, old man, I didn't…"

"You didn't know."

"Want to tell me?"

"Why not?" said Gus, taking a gulp of the bitter-tasting coffee served in the mess. "She's called Bunty. Bunty Kermode. It's Bernice, actually, but Bunty suits her well. I met her in September 1940. She delivered a Hurricane to a Polish squadron I was with."

"She was with the Air Transport Auxiliary?"

"That's right. Anyway, one of the Poles tried it on a bit with her, and Bunty gave him a good roasting. Well, after that, I just couldn't resist her."

"How did she come to be in a wheelchair?"

"Bad crash. She was a lone pilot in a Whitley and came down in poor visibility. There was an engine fire. Anyway, she managed to avoid going down over a town and put the Whitley down in a field, but got badly beaten up herself in the process. Broken back."

"How bad is it?" asked Paddy.

"That's what I'm going to find out."

Bunty was waiting for Gus on the platform at Gloucester station. His eyes widened when he saw her.

"You can stand? Why didn't you tell me the good news?" he blurted.

Bunty wrapped her arms around him. Then, easing her grip, she looked into his face. "Can't you work that out for yourself, Gus?"

"Perhaps you wanted to know if I'd come, assuming you were still in a wheelchair. Is that it?"

She nodded. "I needed to know if you'd still want me in that way, Gus. Do you understand what I'm talking about?"

"Yes. C'mon, let's go for a drink."

They slowly walked to a nearby pub. Gus ordered a pint of bitter. "What will you have, Bunty?"

"Just a lemonade, please. I'm still on medication and Percy says it doesn't mix well with alcohol."

"Percy?"

"My doctor. Percy Dickens."

"On first-name terms, then?"

"Are you jealous?"

"No. But it's a bit unusual, first-name terms with a doctor. What is he — air force, army, or a civilian?"

"Civvy."

"Attractive?"

"Yes. Sort of."

"Married?"

"You are jealous, aren't you? Well, fancy that! Bouncy boy is jealous of a civvy doctor! Now, isn't that sweet?"

Gus blushed. She was right, of course. He was jealous. But why?

"No, Percy isn't married, if you must know. Do I like him? Yes. Would I sleep with him? Probably. But not while I have you. I do have you, Gus, don't I?"

"Yes, of course you do. I'm all yours," he said, a flush coming to his cheeks again.

"Then you can safely put Percy Dickens out of your mind. All right?"

"All right. I won't mention him again. Tell me what happened."

"Percy said my recovery is a miracle. I wrote to him on the first of April, wishing him good fortune and telling him I could stand, unaided, and walk a few paces. He thought it was an April Fool, but the following week he visited me at home. He said he couldn't explain it in medical terms."

"Perhaps the doctor misdiagnosed?"

"Perhaps he did. And the other doctors. But I think it was a case of mind over matter. I wanted my legs to work again and I can be very strong-willed when I want to be! Once my legs started moving, I practised limping from one side of the room to the other."

Gus smiled. Bunty never failed to surprise and impress him. She was one of the most positive people he'd ever met.

"Percy told me that if I carried on making progress, I'd be walking, maybe with a limp, within weeks. I told him I didn't intend to have a limp."

"You don't have a limp," said Gus.

"Even so, the Air Transport Auxiliary won't sanction me flying again, Bouncer! I was interviewed by a stern-faced officer who told me she might be able to find me a desk job somewhere. I don't want a boring desk job, so I told her, 'No thanks, that's not for me.' And do you know what she said to me?"

"Go on."

"She said, 'Then please hand your uniform back as soon as possible, Miss Kermode.'"

"Oh no! What did you say to that?"

"I said I'd take the bloody thing off now and walk back to the station in my underwear, if she liked. And did she scowl! She said that wouldn't be necessary and that next week would be adequate — they'd even reimburse me the cost of postage."

Gus had to laugh at that.

"I told her that wouldn't be necessary, stood up, saluted, and walked to the door. Then I left the offices of the Air Transport Auxiliary for good." Bunty looked up and Gus saw tears forming in her eyes. He knew how much she had loved her work with the ATA.

"What will you do now? Work wise?"

"I just don't know."

"Desk work is necessary, you know. It's all vital war work, Bunty."

71

"Yes, I know. But I need to do something more interesting than organising delivery flights."

"Look, I have an idea. I have a contact in Special Ops — it's very hush-hush and I can't tell you much. But I can put a word in for you, if you like?"

"I'm not fit enough to go parachuting behind enemy lines, if that's what you have in mind. And I may never be."

"No, but there's plenty of other work. Behind the scenes work, undercover work. It may be based at a desk — I don't know. But it's closer to the war, and it's very, very important."

"I haven't spotted any advertisements for it."

"No. They don't advertise."

"So how do they recruit?"

"Recommendations. Friends of friends. A bit like this, I suppose."

She thought about it for several seconds. "And you can put a word in for me?"

"Yes."

"Well, then, yes. If you'd do that for me, I'd be very grateful, Bouncy," she said. "Oh, do forgive me, I haven't even asked about you. How are things up in the great blue yonder?"

"Good. I passed the basic training and am heading to my new unit. I'm about to be dined in, as a matter of fact. Can't invite you, though. Sorry. Men only."

CHAPTER 12

A few days later, Gus looked around at the other officers, all of them wearing the smartest version of their RAF uniforms. The men wore blue air force jackets, with large grey lapels, gold buttons and gold braid around the cuffs, as well as tight trousers and waistcoats. Everyone wore white shirts and black bowties. Gus thought they looked odd, then remembered he was dressed exactly the same way. He'd volunteered in the early days of the war and, as a qualified pilot, had headed straight for the Auxiliary Air Force. This was when his mother had bought him the expensive mess dress in the hope he might have a regular opportunity to wear it. So far, he had not.

This new unit, however, had decided to keep up traditions, and had organised a dining-in night at RAF Tempsford's officers' mess to welcome him and Paddy. They met in the mess bar for cocktails. Gus and Paddy ordered whisky and sodas and took then into a corner. Then Gus saw the commanding officer walk into the bar with Peacock. What on earth was he doing here?

When dinner was called, Gus entered the dining hall and, along with everyone else, stood formally behind his chair until the senior officer present — in this case the station commander, a group captain — entered and seated himself. Flying Officer Benson, one of the youngest present who had been nominated Mr Vice for the event, invited the chaplain to say grace and the dinner began. Gus found himself seated between a squadron leader and a flight lieutenant, both much more senior than himself. The flight lieutenant introduced himself as Thomas Hopwood.

"Where were you before joining us, Bouncer?" he asked.

"I came directly from attachment to a Polish SOE squadron. Halifax bombers. I was navigating, not flying the kite."

"And prior to that?"

"Well, I flew Lysanders over France in 1940."

"Ah, reconnaissance, was it? Just what the Lizzie was built for."

"That's right."

"Plenty of experience with them, then. What would you say is the best feature of a Lysander?"

Gus thought for a moment, chewing on white bread smeared with bloater paste. "It's got to be its low-speed handling. Those automatic slats working the flaps are a dream. The pilot just doesn't need to worry about it and can concentrate on everything else that's going on."

"Well, I can't fault you there, old boy," said Hoppy. "Good cockpit visibility for reconnaissance, too."

"Agreed."

"Flown anything else in action?"

"Fighters: Gladiators, Hurricanes, Spits and Defiants."

"Goodness, you've been around and about a bit, then?"

Gus grinned. "You could say that."

"How's the food, Bouncer?" interrupted the CO.

"Very good, sir," lied Gus, remembering the delights produced by Aircraftsman Wonnacott, the cook-cum-mess orderly at RAF West Malling back in his Defiant-flying days.

"Anything else?" said Hoppy, continuing his interrogation. Gus realised that Paddy was getting a similar grilling from his table companion.

"Yes, actually. I've flown Blenheims and a delivery run on Beaufighters. Oh, and there was that Italian Breda I stole and took over to Crete," he replied, deciding to lay it on thick.

As the evening wore on, the food, Gus noticed, was largely ignored as more and more wine, beer and spirits were consumed by the officers assembled. After pudding, port was placed on the table. Once all glasses were charged, Mr Vice stood and tapped the table for attention. "All stand for the loyal toast," he commanded.

They all stood and raised their glasses.

"To the king," called Benson.

"To the king," echoed the room.

Following a short break, during which some poor quality, bitter coffee was served, the CO stood.

"Gentlemen, I give you our guest of honour, Wing Commander Sir Alexander Peacock, who has driven from London to address us this evening. Over to you, Sir Alex." The CO turned to Peacock and resumed his seat.

Peacock rose slowly and began his speech. "Gentlemen," he began, "the war has turned a corner. As you know, just before Christmas, the Japanese launched an outrageous and unprovoked attack on Pearl Harbor, following which Germany and Italy declared war on the USA. This was a grave mistake by our adversaries. Since then, America has declared war on Germany and in January this year the first US troops arrived in Britain. We welcome our allies with open arms and the kind words, 'better late than never'…"

Raucous laughter filled the dining hall.

"The fall of Singapore is indeed a setback, but we will return, mark my words. Here in Europe things are turning our way. In February, men of the newly formed 1st Airborne Division went into action for the first time. Their target was the German Würzburg radar installation at Bruneval. Then in March an audacious Combined Operations raid on the port of

St Nazaire in German-occupied France was carried out. Packed with tons of high explosives, the destroyer HMS *Campbeltown* was rammed into the gates of the only dry dock capable of servicing the German battleship *Tirpitz*. Such was the damage that the dry dock has been rendered unusable. We hope it will remain so for the remainder of the war.

"Combined Operations are planning further, larger and more damaging incursions into enemy-held territory as we speak. And this is where your gallant contributions come in. Intelligence is vital to the success of our work, and the dangerous missions you fly are key to that intelligence. So, gentlemen, carry on with your gallant operations in the knowledge that your king and country are depending on you and will be most grateful to you when this war is won."

At the end of his speech, Peacock toasted the squadron, and sat down to vigorous applause. Then the assembly moved back to the bar.

"How's everything going, Gustaw?" asked Peacock, who had sidled up to him, carrying a glass of gin. Gus thought it looked like a double measure.

"So far so good," he replied.

"Well," said Peacock, "I'm sorry to put a spanner in the works, but I need you in London next week. There's going to be an inquest into that bloody Lodz affair that went so badly." He moved away before Gus could ask any questions.

Shortly after Peacock left, a raucous game of football commenced, using a white cabbage from the kitchen as the ball. Soon the mess floor became slippery with bits of cabbage. The game was followed by a piggyback fight.

"Come on, Bouncer, climb onto my shoulders!" called Paddy. "We'll soon show them!"

Gus felt that he really didn't have the energy for it, but Paddy insisted. As luck would have it, they lost the first round and Gus was able to slip away to his room.

CHAPTER 13

"Flight Lieutenant Beaumont, would you please tell us exactly what happened?" said Sir Alexander Peacock.

"The mission was betrayed. That's what happened," cut in Krawiec before Gus could respond, banging his fist on the large desk. They were seated in Sir Alex's office in Baker Street.

"Calm down, Piotr," said Peacock. "We don't know that for sure. That's why we're here." He looked at Gus. "I've brought Gustaw down from Tempsford because he was there on the mission. Now, I repeat, please tell us exactly what happened."

"We approached the DZ at two hundred and fifty feet. The pilot, Flying Officer Błaszczykowski, had lowered the flaps and we were flying as slowly as he dared — about sixty-five knots. I went to the back to wish the men good luck. Almost as soon as I got there, the red light came on. When it changed to green, the dispatcher sent them all down the Joe hole and I watched the chutes open. Then the pilot turned for a second run and the same dispatcher chucked out the supplies. I went back to the cockpit. Before I got there, he was shouting that we'd been betrayed. There was nothing we could do. Błaszczykowski turned to port so we could try to see what was going on. All I saw were shots coming towards the parachutes from the ground surrounding the drop zone. There was no returning fire."

"They were killed in their chutes!" shouted Krawiec. "They didn't stand a chance. When I find out who betrayed my men, I'll kill the bastard!"

"Gustaw, who knew the location of the drop zone?" asked Peacock.

"Squadron Leader Krawiec, Squadron Leader Grindlethorpe, and myself."

"The pilot? Błaszczykowski?"

"No, sir. I only told him the route to fly once we were airborne."

"Piotr, how many of the partisans on the ground knew?"

"I informed only the cell leader. I don't know how many others knew."

"And what do they think happened?"

"They believe somebody here in London tipped off the Germans. They lost seven of their own people on the ground, alongside the agents."

"Who on earth would tip off the Germans?" asked Peacock.

"My bet is that sly bastard, Grindlethorpe," growled Krawiec.

Eventually, Peacock managed to placate the Pole, who left at eleven o'clock. Grindlethorpe knocked on Peacock's office door thirty minutes later. They sat around the desk with a pot of tea, three cups and a small milk jug between them.

"Piotr Krawiec thinks we've got a double agent here in London, Titus," said Peacock. "What do you think?"

"Nonsense!"

"Milk?"

"Yes, please."

"He thinks it might be you, Titus. He thinks you tipped off the Germans."

Grindlethorpe started, spilling hot tea down his trousers. "Utter bloody nonsense! Why on earth would I do that?"

"That's what I thought," said Peacock. "But I've been looking into your history, old boy. Supporter of Oswald Mosley, weren't you? Back in the day?"

Gus looked up briefly at the mention of the notoriously fascist MP.

"What if I was?" Grindlethorpe retorted. "Doesn't make me a bloody spy!"

"No, of course not."

"Anyway, Sir Alex, how does Krawiec know it was the Germans that were tipped off? Beaumont and the crew didn't see anyone on the ground, did you, Flight Lieutenant?"

"That's correct, sir. I only saw gunfire."

"What if it was the Reds? What did Krawiec call them? The Armia Ludowa. What if somebody tipped off the Communists?"

"So, you do agree with Piotr? You think somebody betrayed the operation? Someone in London?"

"Well, there could be a traitor, I suppose."

"And who, here in London, would betray loyal Poles to the Communists? And why?"

Grindlethorpe's eyes flicked to Gus and then back to Peacock. "Sir Alex," he said, "what I have to say on this matter is absolutely confidential, and I will not divulge it with the flight lieutenant in the room."

"Gustaw, please would you leave us for a while? Take your tea with you and sit in the common room. I'll send for you when Squadron Leader Grindlethorpe and I have finished."

Gus got up, picked up his cap and cup of tea and left the room. He closed the door, leaving the two older men in conversation. He walked downstairs, sat in a comfy armchair and had a glance through the newspaper. After twenty minutes, a corporal came in and escorted him back to Peacock's office. Grindlethorpe was still there.

"Sit down, Gustaw," said Peacock.

Gus knew from the wing commander's tone that something was wrong.

"Both Squadron Leaders Krawiec and Grindlethorpe believe somebody tipped off the Germans. Now, we really need to be sure of one or two things. First of all, tell me, do you know if it was the Germans doing the shooting at the Lodz drop zone? Could you see?"

"No, sir. All we saw were flashes from the ground around the drop zone."

"Might it have been the Communists? The Armia Ludowa? Piotr says they hate the London Poles."

"Well, yes. I suppose it may have been, but we'll never know. We couldn't see anyone."

"You said the Halifax was very low, Gustaw."

"Yes, and it was pitch-black. We saw nothing of the ground."

"And you are sure — absolutely sure — that you didn't divulge details of the drop zone, even inadvertently, to anyone?"

"Of course I'm sure, Sir Alex. What is all of this about?"

Peacock stood up and looked towards Grindlethorpe. "Thank you, Titus," he said. "I have some business to discuss with the flight lieutenant."

Giving Grindlethorpe time to get out of earshot, he said, "Gustaw, let's go through this, just the two of us. Krawiec seems to think Grindlethorpe may have betrayed the mission to the Germans. What do you think of that?"

"Why on earth would he? It doesn't add up."

"Funny, that's also what Grindlethorpe said. Why on earth would he? Anyway, there's something else."

"Yes, sir?"

"Squadron Leader Grindlethorpe thinks *you* might have tipped off the Reds."

"Me? But that's utter bloody nonsense! What did he say, exactly?"

"He reminded me that your mother is a communist and a well-known friend of Rosa Luxemburg. Was she a friend of your mother?"

"Róża Luksemburg, to use the Polish pronunciation, was born in Poland. She became a German citizen later on. She was, indeed, a friend of my mother before the last war, Sir Alex — Rosa was killed in 1919!"

"Titus seemed to know an awful lot about your family background. He had a more than healthy interest, one might say. But he insists that if someone here in London tipped off anyone in Poland, then the most likely candidate is you."

"Do you think I'm a traitor, Sir Alex?"

"No."

"Do you think Squadron Leader Grindlethorpe is a traitor?"

"No, I don't, though anything is possible. Now, tell me, Gustaw, what do you think happened?"

"I think Squadron Leader Krawiec is wrong. Nobody in London tipped off the Germans or the Armia Ludowa. It was one of their own. Perhaps one of them was captured and tortured…"

"Unlikely. They'd have called off Operation Lodz if they thought they'd been exposed."

"Then either somebody did it deliberately, perhaps for money, or they were simply lax. Or it was just bad luck. But I don't believe for one minute that a tip-off came from this end."

"Thank you, Gustaw. That's what I think, too. But how to convince Krawiec?" Peacock paused, frowning. "What did you just say, Gustaw? Either somebody did it deliberately, for money, or…"

"Or they were lax, not vigilant enough."

"No — I think it's money. I thought something wasn't right. It's been nagging at me for weeks now. Rents in the centre of town are extortionate — that's why I took the flat in Pinner. So how does Grindlethorpe afford to live near Regent's Park? He must have a source of funds. Where does he get the money?"

"Sir Alex, however much I dislike the man, I find it difficult to believe Squadron Leader Grindlethorpe is a traitor."

"Thank you, Gustaw. You may leave now. Oh, one minute. I have a little request — it might turn out to be a job for you, Gustaw, if you fancy it?"

Gus hesitated. Peacocks 'jobs' were usually bad news. "Sir?"

"We want to test a Lockheed Hudson for moonlight ops."

"Lockheed Hudsons? Can they land and take off on short strips?"

"That's exactly what I want you to find out."

"I'll chew on it, if I may, sir. I've got my first operational sortie coming up soon. I need to concentrate on that."

Gus put on his grey RAF side cap, saluted and walked towards the door. Lodz had been a disaster. How far it would set the Polish SOE back was anyone's guess.

CHAPTER 14

Gus clambered into the cockpit and went through the usual checks. After many training flights, these checks were becoming instinctive — all the more reason for double-checks. His hand felt for the tail trim wheel. Good, it was fully forward.

161 Squadron pilots usually spent the week before and the week after each full moon at Tangmere. Gus had his target two days before the planned flight. This gave him plenty of time to prepare his course to a field to the east of the River Saône, northeast of Mâcon. He used this time to cut numerous strips from a 1:500,000 scale map; each strip had his planned route in the middle and around fifty miles on each side. Gus taped the strips together to make a single linear map, which he then carefully folded so that he could hold it in one hand and study it whilst flying. Then he made up his cards with navigational data for each leg of the trip, and taped these onto the blank part of his linear route map showing the English Channel. For the area around the target, Gus followed the same procedure but with a 1:250,000 map that gave much more detail.

His briefing folder also contained some air reconnaissance photos of the field and the area close to it. These had been taken by high-flying Spitfires of the Photographic Reconnaissance Unit operating out of RAF Benson, and Gus was grateful for them.

On the night of the flight the Met Office had forecast a chance of fog on low-lying ground around the target area, but the decision was made to go anyway. Gus was wearing a mixture of RAF uniform and civvies. A dark blue rollneck sweater under his battledress top would not only keep him warm on the flight, but could help him blend in with French civilians if he had to ditch the Lizzie. Civvy shoes and a beret were stashed in the locker along with a standard pilot's escape kit, containing a cloth map, a compass and a wad of French banknotes. He also carried a Webley revolver.

Gus started up the engines and a gave a thumbs-up to the ground crew. He watched as one of them removed the chocks, then he taxied the Lysander to the end of the strip. With the brakes fully applied, Gus pushed forward on the throttle lever and heard the roar of the powerful Bristol Mercury engine. Once it was almost up to maximum prop speed, he let off the brakes and the Lizzie raced along the strip, picking up speed. Gus eased back on the stick and the Lysander climbed away, heading due west. Leaving Tangmere in the distance, Gus turned to port and picked up his first compass bearing, which took him over the Channel. He crossed the French coast through one of the narrow, flak-free corridors that RAF reconnaissance had picked out. Then he altered course and steered towards Nantes.

Eventually, Gus picked out the moonlit Loire. He turned to port and followed the river as far as Tours. From here the route was to be navigated by dead reckoning. Gus turned to starboard until his compass showed him heading due south. He had to fly exactly forty-five miles on this course to pick up the landing zone, a field just south of the village of Descartes. He reduced his speed to two hundred and eight knots and looked at his watch.

Ten minutes later, Gus saw the flashing light in the distance, about half a mile away.

Dot dot dot dash, dot dot, dash dot dash dot. Vic. The codeword. They could hear the Lysander's engine.

He steered the plane towards the flashing light. Using the underwing light, Gus signalled the corresponding letter. Dot dot dash dot. F.

The instant he did so, the flashing from the ground ceased and new lights appeared — orange flares tinged with white. These new lights marked out an L shape. A solitary light marked the top end of the longer side, which Gus knew would be about a hundred and fifty yards — more than enough for the Lysander. Two more flares, closer together, marked the shorter edge of the L shape and the end of usable landing room. This was the makeshift landing strip Gus was aiming for.

He was approaching downwind and overshot the strip, so he turned and put the Lysander onto a new approach. He was now heading towards the two flares marking the shorter edge, flying parallel with the longer side of the L. So long as the agent on the ground had done his work well, this would head Gus into whatever wind there was down there.

He slowed the aircraft to fifty knots, the automatic wing slats and slotted flaps adjusting to prevent the Lysander stalling as he did so. He touched down midway along the strip towards the two flares that marked the bottom of the inverted letter L. Gus turned around between the two flares, taxied back to the opposite end of the strip and turned again. As Gus set the tail trim wheel for take-off, a figure came running out of the woods on the port side of the Lysander.

"*Bonsoir, monsieur.* A good landing, but your passengers are not yet here. You'll have to switch off the engine and wait."

"No way, *monsieur*! I'll keep it running," Gus replied.

He was worried. The Lysander was usually started by a trolley-based battery pack, operated by RAF groundcrew. It had a small, internal battery on which the engine could be started, though these were prone to running down very quickly. It was safer to keep the engine ticking over.

"If you insist, but they'll be twenty minutes at least."

Gus sweated as he waited, tapping nervously on the joystick. Twenty minutes? How much fuel would that use up? He was deep behind enemy lines, relying on Resistance fighters he'd never met to keep a good lookout for any approaching Germans. He was totally at the mercy of the efficiency of these unseen men and women of the Maquis.

At last, Gus spotted the headlights of an approaching vehicle.

"Is this them?" he shouted above the engine's roar.

"I hope so, *monsieur*," said the Frenchman, releasing the safety catch on his Sten gun.

It was a car, nothing else. It stopped and three people quickly got out and came around the rear of the Lysander to the port side. A man was the first to climb the Lysander's ladder. At the top he turned and beckoned to the others. Three suitcases were passed up to him. Then a woman and another man climbed up the ladder and into the cockpit.

"Ready?" asked Gus, over his shoulder.

"Two boxes in the boot of the car," said a man with an English accent.

Gus looked towards the car. Sure enough, the Resistance fighters on the ground were manhandling two large boxes.

"What's in them?" asked Gus.

"Sorry. Can't possibly tell you, old boy. But needless to say, it's frightfully important stuff."

"We won't fit them in. If the boxes are so bloody important, you'll need to leave a couple of suitcases behind."

His three passengers quickly debated the situation. Two of the suitcases were opened, and hands dived into them. Gus, his back to the three agents, couldn't see much of what was going on.

"Get a bloody move on!" he bellowed.

Two suitcases were thrown from the Lysander's cockpit and the boxes hauled up. Gus waved to the man on the ground. With the brakes on hard, he pushed forward on the throttle lever to open up the engine. Once it was almost up to maximum prop speed, Gus checked the tail trim wheel again, then let off the brakes. The Lysander was soon airborne and Gus gained height and headed north, toward the French coast.

"There's a flask of tea and some biscuits in a pouch there," he shouted back to the Joes in the rear of the cockpit. "Help yourselves."

The flight home was the exact reverse of Gus's route out. Ten minutes north of the pick-up was the city of Tours. He turned to port and followed the Loire to Nantes. From there, a course of fifteen degrees magnetic would take him east of the Cherbourg Peninsula and English Channel to Tangmere.

He hit the cold front midway through the homeward flight. There was simply no way around it. As the Lysander flew into cloud and rain, Gus could make out the darker shapes of cumulonimbus clouds partially concealed within the bad weather.

"We're about to be bumped around a little," he said. "Better hold on tight."

Within minutes, the Lysander was being tossed around the sky like a leaf by the strong draughts created by the weather front. There was a flash of lightening which blinded him. Ice was building up on the wings, forcing the Lysander to lose height. Then they emerged on the other side and were over the Channel.

Once they were on the ground at RAF Tangmere, a vehicle came to pick up the Joes. Gus made his way to the cottage. There he was debriefed by an intelligence officer.

"It went well," said Gus. "No flak on the way out. On the way home, the weather was so bad nobody on the ground would have been able to see or hear the engine."

"Any comments?"

"It was a struggle to squash the Joes in, and we had to leave some things behind. The Lysander just isn't big enough for multi-pick-ups. In my opinion, we need larger aircraft."

"That's what I think, too," said the intelligence officer. "We'll have to come up with something different."

And this, thought Gus, *is exactly why Peacock wants the Hudson to be trialled.*

CHAPTER 15

Since he had a few days' leave, Gus met his cousin Staś Rosen for afternoon tea in a London tearoom — not the one off Greek Street.

"My God, Gus, I'm telling you, the Germans' Focke-Wulf is some machine! Even our Spits can't catch them. This Fw-190 could change everything up in the air."

Gus knew that Staś was not exaggerating. His cousin was a vastly experienced fighter pilot who'd fought the Germans in the skies above Poland, France and England. Staś had flown PZL P-11s, Morane-Saulnier 406s and, in the Battle of Britain, both Hurricanes and Spitfires. He'd been involved in many a dogfight against Bf-109s and 110s, blasting a good number of them out of the sky.

"I've never come across a fighter as fearsome as these Focke-Wulfs," Staś went on. "They're fast, manoeuvrable and, boy, can they climb!"

"You're at Biggin Hill nowadays. That's right, isn't it?"

"Yes. I took command of a flight of Spitfire Vs there — an all-Polish outfit."

"Any of the other chaps with you?"

"Butch Paderewski and Max Bartoszyn are there. Butch has been promoted and Max recommended for the DFC."

"Tell me more about these Fw-190s."

"One morning last week, we'd been ordered over the Channel 'to entice the Luftwaffe fighters and engage them in combat.'" Staś smiled. "Those were the exact orders. So very English, don't you think?"

"Very. Go on."

"You see, since September the Germans haven't been so keen on getting up into the air and fighting us."

"Why should they? The war's turned to North Africa and Russia. Why risk lives and machines in meaningless exercises in Europe?"

"Absolutely. They've got enough work now we've begun bombing raids. But it had to come to an end one day. Well, we're on the receiving end of that. I ordered the flight up to angels fifteen as we approached the French coast in a finger-four formation. 'Bandits below, eight o'clock, skipper,' called Max. I looked down and fixed them in my sights. The Abbeville Boys had come out to play — four single-engined fighters. Bf-109s, I supposed. Well, at first I didn't even think about it. Whatever they were, they were covered in swastikas and black crosses — these were the same Nazi bastards who had attacked our homeland. They'd killed Tunio and I was going to attack them.

"I ordered the flight to wheel around to port and to follow me. They stuck to me like glue. I pulled my Spit into a location where we could attack out of the sun, then glanced sideways to make sure the other three were with me and we were in the best position. They were. I called out the 'tally-ho!' and thrust the Spit into a steep dive towards the Germans. As I swept down, I had a good view of the aircraft. They weren't 109s like I thought. They were about the same size as a Messerschmitt single-seater, slender and with square-edged wings, but they had what looked like radial engines and a bubble-type canopy over the cockpit.

"I picked out a target, the penultimate German. I told Butch, who was flying as my wingman, to take the bastard at the back and ordered the others to be ready to pick up the pieces. You know what it's like, Gus; most RAF pilots open fire far too soon. Not me. Not my flight of Poles. Down we swept, gaining on the unsuspecting Luftwaffe pilots. They were about fifteen hundred feet below, ahead and slightly to the right of us. I opened the throttle even further and closed the gap between me and the German aircraft. I reached point-blank range and pushed the fire button. The vibration of that two-second burst shook the Spit violently. I kept her nose firmly aimed at the target, watched the tracer, and saw it hit the tailplane. There were strikes all along the port side of the plane. A piece of metal flew off the engine cowling as the German aircraft rolled away, smoke pluming from it. *Now for the next one*, I thought. I turned to get a view of the melee. Butch was chasing one of the German fighters. Another Spitfire closed in on a German. I aimed at my second target and opened fire, but he turned away and I missed. I watched as he picked up speed. As he continued to port, I saw Italian markings under the cockpit."

"What?"

"I'm bloody sure of it, Gus. I saw a bright blue roundel with one of those axe things painted on it. Brown handle, silvery-white blade."

"A *fasces*," said Gus.

"What's that?"

"Originally it was the symbol of the authority of the Roman Republic. Mussolini adopted it with the same meaning in mind: supremacy of the state. You're right; the marking is unmistakenly Italian. Are there Italian pilots fighting in the Luftwaffe?"

"Don't ask me. Anyway, the German aircraft were obviously returning to base, so I ordered my lads to follow them. We gave chase. I followed the fighter with the Italian markings. That pilot was good. He put his plane into a stiff climb. I followed, but I just couldn't catch him. The Spit simply couldn't close the gap."

"Sounds ominous," said Gus. "Hurricanes will have a real struggle."

"Not a chance in hell, I'd say. When we got back to base, I asked Lech Lewandowski, our intelligence officer, what the bloody hell they were. 'Fw-190s,' he said. 'The Germans call them Würgers.' Which in English translates as shrike — a butcherbird. It's superior to a Spit V in just about everything: speed, rate of climb, and firepower. But he did say that he'd been told the Spit still has the edge in a tight turn. Apparently, an Fw-190 came down at RAF Pembrey in South Wales a few weeks ago, perfectly intact. A German pilot mistakenly landed there, thinking he was in France."

"Nonsense!"

"Apparently it's true. He even waggled his wings in a victory celebration before lowering the undercarriage and landing. Korczak was in on the interrogation. The pilot insisted he'd flown out from Brittany, pursuing a flight of Bostons. He got mixed up with a squadron of Spits over the Channel. Then he was dogfighting over sea and land. He fought his way out then must have got confused, because he was flying north rather than south. He spotted the Bristol Channel, thought Wales was France and landed at Pembrey."

"These Fw-190s don't have a compass, then?"

"Come on, Gus. You know what it can be like."

Gus did know what it could be like. In the adrenalin-fuelled heat of combat, it would be all too easy to make a terrible mistake like that. He'd heard a rumour that in the mayhem of Dunkirk, the commander of a British destroyer had picked up soldiers from the beaches then pulled into Calais, thinking he was in Dover. Anything was possible in this damned war.

"Anyway, the pilot was taken away to Fairwood Common for interrogation and the kite's been tested. The Fw-190 is the easiest modern German aircraft to start up unaided, apparently. It's a simple case of making sure the petrol tap is on and giving it half a dozen pumps on the doper. The starter is pressed down for fifteen seconds to energise and then up to engage. The engine should be warm enough for take-off after moving just a couple of hundred yards on the ground. But like I said, apparently the Spit still has the edge over the Fw-190 in a tight turn."

"Possibly," said Gus, "but fighting them is going to be a real challenge, and you've got to catch the bastards first. You're going to have your work cut out, Staś."

CHAPTER 16

The telephone call from Doctor Harris was as short as it was disturbing. Gus's mother, Magda, had taken a turn for the worse. If he wanted to see her before she died, he needed to get to Winchester as quickly as possible.

When Gus arrived at the house, the doctor was there.

"Am I too late?"

"No," replied Doctor Harris, "she's still with us, but you need to prepare yourself. She doesn't have long."

"Is she conscious?"

"In and out. I've given her some pretty strong pain relief."

"What is the illness, exactly?"

"Her breathing is poor; she certainly has some kind of chest infection. Pneumonia, as likely as anything. But old age and weariness take their toll too, you know. She's never been the same since your father died."

"Thank you for everything you've done for her, Doctor. And for my father, when he was alive."

"It's been a pleasure. I'm just sorry that I can't do more. She's not in pain — at least I could make sure of that. Look, I must be off; I've got other patients to see."

"Of course. Thanks again, Doctor."

As Doctor Harris left, Gus climbed the stairs that led up to his mother's bedroom. He knocked lightly on the door. No response. He knocked again, louder this time. Nothing. He opened the door and crept in.

Magda lay on her bed, her eyes closed. Gus thought she might have died in the short time between Harris leaving her and himself arriving. He crept closer to his mother and heard the low, rattling sound of her shallow breaths. *She's still with us,* he thought.

What to do? Who to tell? In these circumstances, other people he knew might send for a priest or vicar. But his mother, though born a Jew, had led a secular life and had no time for religion. Eunice, who had an excellent relationship with his mother, was uncontactable, away on SOE work. He could phone Staś and ask him to come over. But what good would that do?

With little alternative, Gus simply sat through the long night, waiting for his mother to pass away. This gave him time to reflect.

His mother had lived a full and active life. Born in Poland, as a young woman she had been a friend of Rosa Luxemburg, and, though wealthy, Magda had always campaigned for the rights of women, and she empathised with ordinary people everywhere. She'd met Lionel, Gus's father, at a diplomatic function in Warsaw, and had returned with him to Winchester, where Gus was born.

Strange, thought Gus. He'd been born in this house, as had his father. His father had died here, too. Soon, it seemed, so would his mother. Birth, life and death; laughter and tears. The highs and lows of existence. All had been enacted within the walls of this house.

He looked again at his mother's ashen face. Her eyes were still closed. Slowly, he realised she had stopped breathing. He waited, watching her chest for a hint of movement. After five minutes, he took her hand and felt for a pulse. There was nothing. Magda Beaumont had gone.

He'd have to get Harris back to confirm it, of course, but that could wait until the morning.

Gus went downstairs to the drawing room, found a bottle of port and poured himself a large glass. Tomorrow he would phone Doctor Harris, inform friends and family of Magda's death and arrange the funeral.

Now, it was time to get drunk.

CHAPTER 17

A few days after Magda Beaumont's funeral, Gus and Eunice were sitting at their usual table in their favourite tearoom off Greek Street. Gus ordered a pot of tea and some scones.

"I'm so sorry about your mother, Gus," Eunice said as they waited for the tea to arrive. "I liked her very much."

"Thank you, Eunice," said Gus with a sad smile. "It was a blessing in disguise, really. Mother was suffering, and after Father died she simply didn't want to be here any longer."

"Well, I am sorry and I apologise for not being able to attend her funeral. I'd have liked to — you know that, don't you?"

"Yes, of course."

"I was —"

The waitress arrived with a tray, interrupting Eunice. Gus poured steaming tea into two cups, followed by a drop of milk. Meanwhile, Eunice buttered two scones.

"Was Staś able to make it?" she asked.

"Yes."

"That's good. How is he?"

"He's fine, thanks. He's still flying Spitfires and relishing it."

The record ended. One of the waitresses walked over to the gramophone and changed the disc. Glenn Miller's 'Moonlight Serenade' began to play.

"Oh, I just love this tune," said Eunice. "Let's dance, shall we?"

"You know that the gentleman is supposed to ask the lady, don't you?"

"Go on then, you old fool."

Gus stood. "Would you care to dance, Miss Hesketh?" he asked theatrically.

"Thank you, Mr Beaumont. Yes, I'd simply love to."

As they danced a slow foxtrot, Gus moved his head close to hers. "Have you made a decision about whether to keep working for Peacock?"

"Gus, I was about to explain that I couldn't attend your mother's funeral because I was in France again."

"Oh, I see. Well, I suppose it's good that you've made the decision. Not so good that it puts you in harm's way again. You know that I worry about you?"

"I know, but I simply couldn't turn my back on it, Gus. I have to do something positive to help out with the bloody war."

"Where did you go?"

"Look, Gus, I…"

"Did you ever manage to track down that French agent you worked with? Xavier — was that his name?"

"Xavier Delacroix. Yes — well, yes and no. Xavier was killed. Arrested by the Gestapo and shot."

"I'm sorry."

"He was a good man."

"Did you love him?"

"Love him? God, I don't know. I liked him. As I said, he was a good man."

The music finished. They returned to their table and sat down again. Eunice topped up their teacups.

"What about you? Do you still see that Air Transport Auxiliary girl of yours?"

"Bunty Kermode. She had a bad accident."

"Oh, no. I'm sorry. I didn't realise."

"No reason why you should have known. Yes, Bunty crash-landed a bomber she was delivering — pretty heavily, by all accounts. She was paralysed for a while, but she seems to have made what the medics think is a miraculous recovery. I've seen her a couple of times since."

"Is she in love with you?"

"I think she's fallen for her doctor, as a matter of fact."

Eunice smiled. "So is that the end of it between you two?"

"Probably."

"Are you disappointed? Would you still like to see her?"

Gus picked up his cup and sipped some of the lukewarm tea. It was now or never, he decided. "Actually, no. I'm going to see her again and explain that there can be nothing but friendship between us. I'd like you to meet her. I think the two of you would get along."

"I'm not sure. From the little you've told me about her, we don't sound very much alike."

"That's true. I hadn't thought about it. Bunty is very … effusive. You're harder to work out."

"Oh, Gus. You make me sound terrible!"

"No. Not at all. Actually, if there's anyone I'd like to be seeing, Eunice, it's you."

She smiled and offered him her hand. Gus took it and gave it a gentle squeeze.

"I'd like to be seeing you too," she said.

"Would you like to have dinner tomorrow?" he asked. "We can dine at the mess. It's not that bad in there these days."

"Oh, you make it sound so lovely! But yes, Gus. I'd love to."

The next day, the food was average — Brown Windsor soup, lamb chops with spring greens, and rhubarb with custard for pudding. Eunice's dress, on the other hand, was simply delightful. It was short-sleeved and gathered at the waist with a belt, falling just below her knees. The colours suited her well — navy blue, with a white collar and four white buttons down the front. Gus could tell the other officers were taken by Eunice, and he felt proud.

After dinner, they sat in the bar over drinks — whisky for Gus and a glass of Madeira for Eunice.

"I'm a bit surprised they can still get this stuff," said Eunice.

"Well, Portugal's neutral, and I think lots of refugees and escapees come through that way. And Joes, no doubt. I bet they bring some of the stuff with them. Better not ask questions though, eh?"

"Agreed. Have you ever thought about what you might do after the war, Gus?" she asked.

"I don't like to think of it. It tempts fate."

"Oh, don't be silly."

"Well, I always thought that I wanted to be a historian."

"Oh, how dull, Gus — swotting over boring, dusty tomes and giving dry lectures. Anyway, it just doesn't suit you any longer."

"Doesn't it?"

"No, you've changed. Or perhaps it's better to say the war has changed you. Nowadays you're always getting yourself into scrapes. I like that very much. It makes you a bit of a wildcard."

"Well, as it happens I think I agree with you. So what about politics?"

"Yes, that's more like it. But you have a problem there as well."

"Do I?"

"Yes. You're the son of a British diplomat and an upper-middle-class Polish woman, for goodness' sake. You are literally a born Conservative…"

"Let me remind you that my mother was proudly left-wing. But, yes, they were rather upper-class, I suppose."

"There's no 'suppose' about it, Gus. But I remember you had some time for the Liberals at Oxford, and that Labour man. Grammar schoolboy, northern accent. What was his name?"

"You mean Harold Wilson?"

"That's the one."

"He was a lecturer at New College. That's where we met. I had many a chat with Harold about politics. He volunteered for military service, but they wouldn't have him. They classed him as a specialist and moved him into the civil service instead."

"Do you keep in touch?" asked Eunice.

"Not really. We weren't that close; we just discussed politics."

"I'm sure your mother would have approved. She was more of a socialist, wasn't she? So just where would you fit in?"

"Labour, I should think. Anyway, what about you? Ever think what you might do after the war?"

"Go back to fashion modelling, I expect."

"Really?"

"Or marry. I think I'll have had enough excitement after all this cloak-and-dagger stuff. But I'll have to find a man who'll have me first."

"Eunice," said Gus, suddenly.

"Yes?"

"Shall we have another drink?"

CHAPTER 18

It was the March full moon. Paddy had taken off from RAF Tempsford and flown down to Tangmere without a hitch. Paddy had been briefed as usual, and had picked up the two SOE agents he was flying to a landing zone just south of the river Loire. With the Joes in the rear cockpit, Paddy had made a textbook take-off and radar had tracked him until he went out of range. He was on course; the sky was clear and conditions for navigation by moonlight were ideal. While no pilot would ever claim these flights were easy, this one should have been relatively straightforward. But Paddy didn't return.

In a close-knit unit like the SOE flight, all losses were heavily felt, and Paddy was a popular, gregarious member of the mess. Gus and his fellow pilots were very sorry to hear that he'd disappeared.

But it seemed that their grief was premature. Two days later, news about Paddy arrived. "He's alive and well — holed up in a Resistance safehouse somewhere close to the original drop," said the squadron leader.

"What on earth's going on?" asked Gus.

"We don't have much to go on. Apparently, Paddy landed all right and on time. He ditched his Joes and they went off to do whatever they do. But Paddy couldn't take off. The Lizzie has been destroyed, and Paddy's in some farmer's attic or something."

"What are we going to do about it?"

"We'll go in and get him. But we can't do it this month — the full moon's behind us. We'll have to wait until the next full moon. I'll get a message over to Paddy and we'll set up a flight. Want to take it on, Bouncer?"

"Yes, I'd love to. I'm keen as mustard to know what the silly bugger's been up to."

On the first night of the April full moon, Gus took off in a Lysander from Tempsford and flew down to Tangmere. He parked the kite up and, whilst it was being refuelled, headed to the cottage for a final briefing. The weather was good, but with a strong south-westerly that would tend to blow him to port, so he allowed for this in his last-minute planning.

There was one Joe to take out — a woman. Gus wondered if she knew Eunice but dared not mention it. SOE pilots speaking to their passengers was severely frowned upon.

"You've got more space than usual," Gus shouted, "so strap yourself in! There's a flask of tea and some biscuits — all we could manage, I'm afraid. Apparently there's a war on."

She smiled nervously. "Thanks, but I'm not hungry."

Gus thought she must be a novice. Perhaps this was her first drop. Poor woman — alone in the back of a flimsy kite piloted by someone she'd never met and bound for a dark field somewhere in France.

"Help yourself if you change your mind," said Gus. "Otherwise, sit back and enjoy the flight. We have perfect conditions. I might ask you to pour me a cup of char about halfway, if that's all right?"

"Yes, of course. Just ask."

Like clockwork, his hand felt for the Lysander's tail trim wheel. Once at altitude, Gus got on course for his landing zone, south of the river Loire.

Once they were over the French coast and had cleared Le Mans, Gus asked for a cup of tea. His passenger fidgeted around and soon produced one. "Here you are. I will have one after all, if that's all right?" she said.

"Of course. Tea always helps, I find."

"Thanks. Have you done much of this before? You seem very capable."

"Well, we've not landed yet." Gus laughed. "Sorry, yes, I've done quite a bit," he lied, not wanting to scare her by letting on that this was only his second SOE sortie. "I flew Lysanders at the beginning of the war, too. In fact, I may have been the first pilot to attack the Jerries in anger — certainly from a Lizzie, like this."

"Really? How spiffing! Do tell."

How much should he tell her? It would take her mind off things, but he didn't want to confess that he still felt responsible for the death of his gunner, Flight Sergeant Chester — for which Grindlethorpe still blamed him — and he certainly wouldn't tell her he'd pranged another Lysander near Calais.

"Well," he began, "I was on a recce run back in May 1940 and we spotted enemy armour coming out of some woods. I rather lost my head and had a go at them. Regular Lysanders have a couple of Brownings fitted to the undercarriage on stub-wings, you see."

"Did you hit anything? Or shouldn't I ask?"

"I did. Got at least one, maybe two of those armed motorcycle combinations. Then I was chased off by a Bf-109."

"Well, good for you. You showed some pluck."

"To tell you the truth, I was reprimanded for it by a pompous old squadron leader. You may have bumped into him in briefings — a chap called Grindlethorpe."

"Oh, none of us like him, actually."

"I'm not surprised. Look, we're going to be losing height soon. Let me pass this back to you, and if you could stow the flask and cups away, that would be a help. Thanks."

Gus put the Lysander into a turn and lost height in a great sweep around where he was sure the landing site was. He soon saw the reception signals from the ground and got the Lizzie on track for the landing field. As he came closer to the ground, he saw that a mist had formed, which made the approach difficult, but after two attempts and a very tight and low circuit, Gus managed to put the aircraft down on the field. He taxied to the end of the strip, turned the kite around and taxied back to the leeward end, turning again to face the Lysander into the wind. As usual, he kept the engine running.

Gus pulled back the cockpit canopy as his passenger climbed onto the portside ladder and began descending. Suddenly she let out a shrill cry.

"What's up?"

"Bloody hell, I caught my ring on one of those sodding notches! Nearly had my finger off!"

"Oh, sorry about that. Are you all right?"

"I'll survive," she said, and blew him a kiss.

He waved. "Good luck."

The woman was whisked away as his old friend Paddy O'Brian climbed hurriedly into the plane and took her place.

"Am I glad to see you, Bouncer!" he shouted as Gus fiddled with the Lysander's tail trim wheel, altering its position for take-off. They waved to the French agents on the ground, then Gus opened the throttle and they were off, soon on a course for Tangmere.

Once up at cruising altitude, Gus shouted to Paddy to put on the RT headphones.

"What the bloody hell happened to you, you daft sod?"

"It wasn't my fault," replied Paddy. "The outward flight and landing were uneventful. However, once on the ground I soon realised that all was not well. The ground was extremely soft. Apparently, they've had a lot of rain recently. I had to give it a great deal of throttle to keep the Lizzie moving. Well, I got to the far end of the strip, but in making the turn to meet the reception committee, she became stuck. The Lysander was immovable even with maximum throttle, and the more I tried the worse it got. Eventually it became bogged down in the mud."

"So you left it?"

"Bugger off! Of course not. First, I got all the people on the ground to push, but that failed. Next, somebody came up with the idea of fetching some bullocks from the nearest farm. Well, in no time at all the farmer arrived with two bullocks. His whole family turned up as well. They were only too keen to help. Someone dug trenches in front of the wheels to form a kind of ramp. The bullocks were hitched to the aircraft, and then we were ready. One, two, three, heave! The bullocks started to pull, but nothing happened. Two more bullocks were fetched, but again the Lysander failed to move. She was totally stuck, Bouncer, going nowhere.

"All of that took about two hours, and I finally realised that there was no hope of digging the aircraft out. So I explained and we set it on fire. The Lizzie burnt well in that misty field, and soon the agents and I were on our way back to a Resistance safehouse, where I was hidden from the Germans until now. How's that for a tale?"

"Paddy, you'll be able to dine out on that story for the rest of your bloody life. Now, you sit back and enjoy the trip. There's tea and biscuits there, if you like."

"Tea and biscuits!" Paddy scoffed. "The French agents sent me away with wine and brandy and some foie gras to share at the mess. Treated me like a king, they did."

In the debrief that followed, Gus mentioned the agent catching her ring on one of the notches that allowed the rear cockpit roof to be stopped partway along the runners. From then on, Joes were ordered not to wear rings; any rings needed for their cover had to be carried in a pocket.

CHAPTER 19

Gus and Bunty met in Hastings, because she didn't want to spend the day in London and he thought the seaside would be nicer. He arrived at ten-thirty and waited for her at the station. Bunty's train was running a little late, getting in at five to eleven. She wasn't up to bounding off the train and along the platform, the way she used to. Instead, Bunty walked slowly towards Gus, and he waved when he saw her.

"You look lovely," he said, admiring her floral summer dress. "How are you?"

"I'm doing just fine, Gus," she replied. "Shall we walk along the prom?"

They did as she suggested. Gus was anxious; he knew he had to sort things out with Bunty, but he didn't know how to raise the subject of their relationship. He valued her friendship and hoped she might feel the same way. Their former desire for each other seemed to have faded. This shift had nothing to do with Bunty's injuries; it had been caused solely by his feelings for Eunice.

After a light lunch at a café on the seafront, they found an isolated promenade seat. Gus glanced around to make sure no one was within earshot.

"How's the work going, Bunty?"

"Good, thanks. Within a month of being interviewed by your friend Peacock…"

"He's not really my friend."

"Well, what is he?"

"He's my senior officer. He was a friend of my father. I first met him in Oxford, before the war. I just happened to bump into him in the Turf Tavern, though now I think it was a set-up. Anyway, I've done some little jobs for him since then."

"Little jobs?"

"You know — espionage."

"Anyway, as I was saying," continued Bunty, "within a month I passed the relevant selection exercises and began training at Bletchley Park in Buckinghamshire."

"Sounds nice."

"There's an old mansion there, but most of us don't work in the big house. It's surrounded by temporary cabins. You know the sort: cold in winter, hot in summer, and always dark and dismal. That's where most of the work goes on."

Gus nodded.

"The conditions are pretty bloody poor, actually. Long hours, and sometimes it gets a bit … over-pressured. I'm in digs with two other girls in Whaddon — that's a small village a few miles away. Mrs Fletcher is our landlady, but she doesn't really want us there, I don't think. There's no inside loo, Bouncer. We have to go out into the back yard. But I shouldn't complain. There's a war on, you know."

"And what is it you're doing there, precisely?" asked Gus.

"You know I can't discuss that, Gus."

"Oh, come on. We've both signed the Official Secrets Act."

"Yes. And it prevents me telling you anything about what I do there."

"But you can tell me if you're typing, filing, or making the tea."

Bunty considered this for a few seconds. "I send and receive Morse code messages."

"Messages to agents?"

"Look, Gus," said Bunty, "if I tell you what goes on at Bletchley then you must promise to keep it a secret. Do you understand? It's more than my life is worth if any of this gets out."

Gus promised not to breathe a word to anyone.

"We decode German messages. The Germans have got some sort of fancy encrypting device and we're part of a team attempting to decipher it." She paused. "It's called an Enigma machine."

"The Poles captured a working Enigma machine," said Gus. "My cousin Staś told me about it."

"We listen in on German wireless messages. They make absolutely no sense, as they are all encrypted. We write them down and send the typed results to a team of decoders. They try to find patterns that will crack the code. But they're always racing against the clock. The Germans will periodically change the code to a completely different one."

"How often do they do that?" asked Gus.

"Every twenty-four hours, at midnight."

"My God. As often as that?"

"Yes. You mustn't say a word about this, but there's a rumour that we will need a machine to crack the codes."

"A machine to break another machine. That makes sense," said Gus.

"I don't work on the codebreaking, by the way. I'm in a team of trained women who spend our days sending and receiving messages in Morse to a spy network. We codename it the Boniface network. The messages are unintelligible, of course. They're encoded to prevent the enemy from knowing the contents if they are ever intercepted."

"And German codebreakers will be working equally hard to crack our codes, I expect."

"I expect so, yes."

The subject of Gus's feelings for Bunty hadn't arisen all day. Somehow, there hadn't been time. Now, they were walking along the seafront and Gus was steeling himself to say something when suddenly the air-raid sirens sounded.

Instinctively, Gus looked out to sea and saw three dots swooping low and coming towards them.

"Spitfires?" asked Bunty.

Gus saw a black dot veer off, and then there was an explosion that threw a column of water into the air behind the pier. The pilot had dropped his bomb too soon.

"Jabos!" Gus shouted. "They must have come in at sea level to avoid our radar. Come on, Bunty! Quick as you can — we've got to find some cover." He took her hand and they began to move.

Gus looked up as another of the German aeroplanes approached. It was coming in fast at about sixteen hundred feet. When it was still about half a mile away, it began a low dive. As it came closer, Gus shouted for everyone around him to lie down.

Gus gazed skywards at the plane and watched as its nose lifted. As the plane began to rise, he got a good view of it. It was a small, single-engined aeroplane with a radial engine. As it climbed out of that shallow dive, it lobbed a single black bomb, which now descended rapidly onto the crowded Hastings promenade. It mattered little, but Gus was now sure the plane was a Fw-190, the new German fighter that Staś had told him about. A Butcherbird.

The aircraft was joined by more Jabos, and suddenly the quiet seaside town Gus and Bunty had arrived to that morning was replaced by chaos as the first explosions echoed through the air. The deafening roar of the bombs drowned out all other sounds. The sky was now full of low-flying aircraft, and scores of people were lying on the ground trying to avoid the strafing machine guns. In an instant, the tranquil neighbourhood had been transformed into a nightmarish scene of smoke, fire, and the cries of the injured.

As Gus lay on the ground, one arm around Bunty, he saw that another Fw-190 was almost above him. The pilot released his bomb and started to bank left. Gus watched as the bomb hit the road and bounced over the railings into the sea. A column of water spouted high into the air. Gus listened as the anti-aircraft fire opened up. Suddenly there was a loud explosion, and he glanced up. One of the 190s had been hit.

Then they were gone. Not a single British fighter had been able to get up into the skies to fight them off. Even if they had, the Focke-Wulfs, once their bombs had been jettisoned, were too fast to be caught. Gus turned to Bunty and felt a sharp pain in his right hand.

"It's all right now, Bunty," he said, "they've gone. Let's see what we can do to help sort this mess."

There was no answer. Gus turned and saw that she was covered in debris.

"Bunty!" he cried, starting to heave the debris off her. He shook her gently, then squeezed her hand. There was no response. Desperately, he searched for her pulse, but felt nothing. Shocked, he closed Bunty's eyes. He didn't want to leave her body, but there was nothing more he could do for her. Heavy with grief and horror, he turned to look at the town.

Panic had set in. The air was thick with the desperate cries of the wounded mingled with the wails of sirens — the all-clear, for what it was worth. A bus driver was screaming from the cab of his vehicle, which was over on its side. Gus leapt to his feet and sprinted over. When he reached the driver, he saw that the man had horrendous injuries to his head and face. "Don't worry, pal," he said. "You're going to be just fine. Stretcher, over here!"

Eventually a first aid crew arrived. The poor man was stretchered away, still screaming.

Gus walked back to Bunty's body. Two firemen and an Air Raid Precautions warden had shifted away the rest of the debris and were preparing to move her.

"Was she with you, mate?" asked the warden.

"Yes, she was," said Gus.

"I'm sorry. You'd better go and talk to that policeman," he said, pointing to a uniformed officer over by the promenade.

Gus passed Bunty's details on to the policeman before he left, telling him that she had an uncle. He didn't mention her doctor, promising himself that he would write to Percy Dickens personally to let him know what had happened to Bunty.

The bus driver's screams and the sight of Bunty lying still on the ground, covered by debris, haunted Gus on the train back to base. He'd never got to talk to her about their relationship, but perhaps she'd guessed his feelings had changed.

When he got back to Tempsford, Gus reported to the medical officer. His hand was now extremely painful, but he'd hardly felt it at the time.

"I was caught in a Jabo raid, Doc. My hand's bloody murder."

"We'll need to get it X-rayed, Bouncer. It might be broken."

The medics strapped up Gus's hand and he was taken by ambulance to the RAF hospital at the Henlow base, just thirteen miles away. X-rays were carried out and confirmed that his right hand was indeed broken. Plaster was applied.

Gus found his short stay at Henlow interesting. As well as being the home of an RAF hospital, Henlow was a repair base for many aircraft types under the direction of No. 13 Maintenance Unit. Numerous aircraft were to be seen on the ground or being flight-tested. Henlow was also used to assemble Hurricanes that had been built at the Hurricane factory operated by Canadian Car and Foundry in Ontario. After being tested in Canada, these aircraft were disassembled and sent to Henlow in shipping containers to be reassembled. A nurse told Gus that over a hundred fitters worked there, and approaching one thousand Hurricanes had been shipped to Henlow from Canada.

Though nothing could take away his grief over Bunty's death, learning more about his temporary lodgings gave Gus something else to think about, and brought a little relief.

CHAPTER 20

Gus had been at Henlow for four days when he received a visit from the senior medical officer.

"Good morning, Flight Lieutenant," he said, smiling at Gus. "I'm pleased to say that you're fit enough to be transferred to a convalescent hospital."

"Thanks, Doc. Where are you sending me?"

"RAF Hospital Torquay, an establishment for officers only. You'll find it much more pleasant there, I'm sure. As you're mobile, we'll get you a rail warrant and send you by train."

Good, thought Gus. The journey to Devon would necessitate a change in London, giving him a chance to see Eunice.

The next day, with the rail warrant in his wallet, Gus clambered into a hospital car, which dropped him at the Arlesey and Henlow station a few miles away. He caught the next train to St Pancras, but try as he might Gus couldn't track down Eunice. Dejectedly, he made his way to Paddington and caught the train to Devon, worrying all the way that Eunice might be back in France doing goodness knew what on Peacock's behalf.

Gus left the train at Torre station, hailed a taxi to take his kit and belongings to the hospital and strolled over to Babbacombe. Torquay in early summer was beautiful.

Arriving at the hospital, he was greeted by an RAF orderly.

"This is a rather grand place," said Gus, gazing up at the facade.

"It is certainly that, sir. The Palace Hotel was requisitioned as a hospital solely for RAF officers. It opened in October 1939, replacing the one in Uxbridge. The clean air, scenic location and easy access are great advantages, sir."

"I'm sure they are."

"And, unlike in Uxbridge, sir, we're all safe here from aerial bombardment. Safe as houses."

"How many patients are there?"

"We have a full complement of two hundred and forty nine beds, sir, all in single rooms. At the moment we have about two hundred officers here. The hospital is staffed by eleven officers, eighty-odd nurses and a similar number of RAF staff like myself. The others are civilian employees. I'll get someone to show you to your room."

Gus's room was clean and comfortable. He found out later that the food was good and there were social events such as dances.

It was time to find out who his neighbours were. Gus looked at the nameplate on the door to the left of his room — Flight Lieutenant James Oscar Stringer-Hislop, RAF — and knocked twice.

"Come in!" shouted a voice.

Gus opened the door and walked in. A young officer was sitting in a wheelchair.

"Hello," he said. "I'm the new boy next door, Gus Beaumont. Bouncer. Pleased to meet you."

Hislop held out his hand. "Likewise, old man. Suppose you read the nameplate — it's a bit of a mouthful. Fellows in the mess call me Josh."

"Ah, I can't shake on it, I'm afraid. My hand is plastered like your leg. How did you break it?"

"Playing rugby against an army team. Well, we are a pair, aren't we? Look, I was just going out for a smoke in the sunshine. Give me a push? I'll tell you all about the place."

"Sure, let's go."

Gus pushed Josh out the door and along the corridor. As they passed the room to the right of his own, he read the nameplate: Flying Officer Hamilton Sampford, RAAF.

"What's he in with? Another broken bone?"

"No. Ham's in with shell shock."

"Shell shock? Do they still diagnose that? I thought it went out with the Great War?"

"Shell shock, neurasthenia, battle-weariness, combat stress reaction — call it what you bloody like, but its real enough."

"Yes, we've probably all seen it, especially in the summer of forty."

"You were in the Battle of Britian?"

"Yes. You?"

"Towards the end, yes. The hospital's well known for its convalescent status, but also for its work in psychotherapy. Cases like Ham, battle-fatigued personnel, are assessed here under a new programme that has evolved since the Great War. During the Battle of Britain, I think the top brass realised the necessity for the rehabilitation of pilots when there was a shortage of experienced aircrew. Here they pay special attention to what they call physio and occupational therapy. Ham will tell you all about it himself."

"How is he doing?"

"He seems all right to me, but I'm no doctor. One thing I disagree with is that they insist on keeping the psychological patients within the hospital grounds. That's why we've got the small bar and the hospital magazine, *The Torquay Tatler*. They seem to think that the bright lights of Torquay might lead to a lapse in the patients' recovery. I disagree. An occasional night on the town does nobody any harm. So some of us sneak them out now and again and have a bit of a pub crawl. Up for a bit of that, Bouncer?"

"Yes. Why not?"

"Good. Then we'll go out tomorrow after tea — you, me, and Ham."

Apart from being rather quiet, Ham Sampford seemed just like any of the vast array of young officers Gus had come across since volunteering for the air force in 1939. He had something of a stammer, but whether this was because of the war, Gus had no idea.

"What unit are you with, Ham?" he asked at tea the following day.

"I-I'm with number 157 Squadron at RAF Castle Camps in Cambridgeshire. Night fighter squadron."

"I used to fly Defiant night fighters," said Gus, "and I did some night fighting in Hurricanes over Malta last year."

"You get about a bit, Bouncer," said Josh. "You're at Tempsford now, you say?"

"That's right. What kites are you flying, Ham?" asked Gus, not wanting to say too much about the hush-hush operations he was involved with.

"Mosquitos."

"Ah, the wooden wonders! Are they as good as they say?"

"They're a good k-kite, yes. H-handle well and certainly f-fast."

"What about you, Josh?"

"I'm with Coastal Command. Based just along the coast in Plymouth. I'm a navigator on Sunderland flying boats. U-boat hunting, convoy support, picking up survivors, that sort of thing."

"Goodness, I can't imagine that. Just you up in the Sunderland and miles of open sea."

119

Later that evening, the three took a walk around the hospital grounds, Ham pushing Josh and Gus walking beside them. They rode down to Oddicombe beach on the tiny funicular railway that careered down the cliffs, then walked along the beach, throwing stones and chatting to some local women who were taking the evening air.

"How about we all go for a drink?" suggested Josh, to nods of agreement and smiles.

The six of them walked up the hill to Babbacombe, sharing the task of pushing Josh up the steep hill, and found a pub. Gus and Ham bought drinks, whilst Josh entertained the young women with stories of his exploits, most of them wildly exaggerated, thought Gus.

After they returned to the hospital, Gus sat alone in his room, thinking it had been a thoroughly pleasant evening. But soon his thoughts switched to memories of Bunty's death and his fears for Eunice.

Gus left Torquay on the 1st of June, a Monday. He bought a newspaper to read on the train and was enthralled by various snippets. In the USA, Italian opera singer Ezio Pinza had been released from Ellis Island after being held on suspicion of being an enemy alien. *Well, he was Italian, but that didn't automatically make him an enemy, surely?* Jews in Nazi-occupied Paris were ordered to wear yellow badges. *Disgraceful.* The German submarine U-568 had been sunk northeast of Tobruk by British destroyers. *Good riddance.* The musical *Yankee Doodle Dandy* starring James Cagney had premiered in New York City. Tickets to the premiere could only be purchased by those who'd bought war bonds. Gus sighed. He thought he'd pay just about anything to be able to go to a picture house with Eunice and watch it.

His eyes flicked down the page. The British had conducted a thousand-plane bombing raid on Cologne, targeting the city's chemical and machine tool industries. Almost fifteen hundred tons of bombs had been dropped in ninety minutes. *And how many civilians killed?* thought Gus. *How many left homeless?*

CHAPTER 21

Gus spent the last four days of his leave in and around Oxford. Murray Parkinson — Eunice's old friend — had invited him to speak about Greece in the Old Library of the University Church of St Mary the Virgin, where Dick Milford was vicar. Gus was surprised to hear from Murray. Although both had been juniors at Brasenose and had been on the same course of study, they'd hardly been close friends. Nevertheless, the opportunity for a few days away from the RAF and the war was appealing. Gus jumped at the chance.

He broke with tradition and wore civvies throughout. Oxford had changed. The city centre had escaped being bombed altogether and none of the medieval college buildings had been damaged. But the war was affecting the university and colleges in other ways. With central London under constant threat of bombing, many government departments had moved to Oxford. While many male dons and students had left to fight, the female government clerks who staffed these departments had migrated to Oxford in large numbers. This gave the city quite a different character.

Some colleges were effectively shut down as their buildings were requisitioned by the military. Colleges that kept going in some manner were the lucky ones, and one such college was Gus's alma mater.

Gus spoke at the church meeting the first night he was in the city. The group he addressed called themselves the Oxford Committee for Famine Relief and had the prospect of a premises on Broad Street. They were an eclectic lot — Quakers such as Murray, social activists and dons. Their overarching aim was to help starving citizens of occupied Greece. Apparently, the country was being plundered of its resources to feed German citizens and troops. The Allied blockade of Greece prevented food from reaching the country. Churchill, said Murray, was in favour of the blockade, arguing that hunger might prompt the Greeks to rise up against the Nazi occupation.

Gus spoke about his time at RAF Menidi near Athens. He told those assembled how he'd crash-landed on the island of Corfu and been saved by the Andartes, the Greek Resistance, and how opposition to the Nazis was strong.

"When the Italians occupied the island in 1923," he said, "the Greek garrison didn't surrender. Rather, the soldiers withdrew to the plains and mountains of Corfu's interior. Those islands lend themselves to guerrilla warfare. The same happened last year, and they're joined by hundreds of civilians."

Gus went on to explain how the Resistance was divided between royalists and communists and how, at least for now, the British government was supporting both.

"How did you get away, Flight Lieutenant Beaumont?" asked one of the audience members.

"I stole an Italian aeroplane and flew it to Crete," he explained, to flabbergasted faces.

"Oh," replied the questioner, surprised. "Well, we can't approve of theft, but well done for escaping."

Gus and Murray popped into the Turf Tavern after the lecture. "Let me get you a drink," said Gus.

"Just a lemonade for me. I'm teetotal nowadays."

Gus brought a pint of ale for himself and the soft drink for Murray and they sat in a quiet corner.

"Have you kept in touch with Eunice Hesketh?" asked Gus, unable to stop himself.

"No. Nothing happened between Eunice and I. I always thought she was still confused over you, as a matter of fact. I believe she took up fashion modelling."

"Yes, she did."

"Do you keep in touch?"

"Not really," lied Gus. "I did bump into her recently."

"And how is she?"

"She seems to be doing all right."

"What is she up to?"

"She didn't really say. Some sort of office work, I think."

"I say, Gus, what would you like to do for the next couple of days?"

"Well, I read Siegfried Sassoon's *Memoirs of an Infantry Officer* at school…"

"Didn't we all?"

"…and I recall that the narrator, George Sherston, Sassoon's alter ego, relaxed by exploring the river Cherwell by canoe. I never got around to doing anything like that whilst studying, but I'd quite like to have a go myself."

"What about your hand?"

"I think it'll be all right, as long as I take it easy. It will be a good test of it, at least."

"In that case, it just so happens that I have a friend who lives in Thrupp. It's a delightful village a few miles north of Oxford, where the river connects to the Oxford Canal. He has a couple of canoes. We could have a bit of a paddle together, if you like. Or maybe you'd like to be alone?"

"No offence, Murray, but alone would be good. A lot to think about, you see."

"None taken. I'll give Johnny — that's my friend over in Thrupp — a bell and see what's on."

Gus spent Tuesday on the river. As he dipped his paddle into the gentle waters of the River Cherwell, a sense of tranquillity enveloped him. It was a delightfully warm summer morning, and already the sun had painted the sky pink and gold, casting a warm glow on the greenery lining the riverbanks.

Navigating the meandering river, taking in the quaint buildings of Thrupp and serene meadows beyond, Gus became lost in thought. He brooded over the war, Eunice and Bunty. Soon the Cherwell had re-joined the canal and at a pub called the Rock of Gibraltar, which amused Gus no end, he stopped for lunch. He bought a pint of ale and a steak and kidney pie and sat beside the canal to eat.

After paddling back to Thrupp, he stayed overnight in Johnny's cottage. Murray's friend was away in London on government business, but had no objection to leaving Gus with a key. There was an old tin bathtub, which Gus filled with hot water, treating himself to a good soak. Afterwards he went into the village armed with a copy of Erskine Childers' *The Riddle of the Sands*, which he'd found on Johnny's bookshelf, and ordered a meal of corned-beef hash at the pub.

The next morning Gus set off to walk back to Oxford along the canal, which wound its way through Kidlington, Summertown and into the Jericho area of Oxford. It reminded him of Bunty and the short time they had spent together on the *Agincourt*, the narrowboat owned by Bunty's uncle Cedric, back in the autumn of 1940.

It was six and a half miles from Thrupp to the end of the canal in Oxford, and at a brisk pace it took Gus just over two hours to get there. Yesterday's canoeing had proved his hand was in good working order, just about. Now the walk proved to Gus his general fitness was good. His body was ready to return to the war, but was his mind? Along the canal he passed numerous workboats carrying goods from the Midlands down to Oxford, most of them horsedrawn. Gus only spotted two diesel-powered boats, and one narrowboat carrying coal was drawn by a mule.

Just as he arrived at the end of the line, a flight of Spitfires flew directly overhead, and Gus was moved by the sound of their Merlin engines. *Yes*, he thought, *I'm ready to get back to the war*.

CHAPTER 22

Gus sat in the pilot's seat of the Lockheed Hudson, a twin-engined, medium bomber. As he razzed the engines in preparation for take-off, he thought how similar the aeroplane was to the Blenheims he had flown over Greece and North Africa.

Built in the USA and based on the Lockheed model 14 Super Electra airliner, the Hudson could easily accommodate eight passengers and so met one of Gus's criteria for an aircraft suitable for pick-ups of larger parties. It also had a reassuringly long range of one thousand, nine hundred and sixty miles, without the need for extra petrol tanks.

The cockpit was roomy with good visibility, and the pilot's seat felt comfortable. The Hudson was about the same length as a Blenheim, but its wingspan was substantially longer. Looking out from the cockpit, Gus guessed each wing to be easily five feet longer on each side. And the Hudson had enormous wing flaps.

Paddy O'Brian was also in the cockpit, taking the navigator's seat. The pair had been sent to the Coastal Command Operational Training Unit at RAF Silloth for a Hudson familiarisation course. On the transport flight to Cumbria, they chatted about the Hudson.

"Having a navigator will take a lot of pressure off the pilot. And we'll take a radio operator."

"Sounds ideal," said Paddy. "There must be a catch."

"Of course there's a catch," replied Gus.

"Go on, tell me."

"The pilot's notes state that the Hudson needs a one-thousand-yard airstrip to land on," said Gus.

"It's probably erring on the conservative side," offered Paddy.

"I bloody well hope so, because we've got orders to land it on a standard SOE three-fifty-yard strip, Paddy."

Before any of this, however, they needed to get the hang of the Hudson. In the cockpit with them was a flying instructor from Silloth, Flying Officer Bert Bridges. The Hudson was easy to handle, though compared to a Lysander there was much more to think about, especially on landing. The pilot's drill was much more complicated than in a Lysander with its fixed undercarriage.

Bridges talked them through the drill. "Check the carburettor air intake is cold. Check the brakes' air pressure feels right and that they're off. Speed must be below a hundred and forty-five knots before lowering the wheels. Check the mixture controls are in auto-rich and the prop controls are fully forward. Superchargers in M ratio. Flaps partly down at first, then fully. Got all that?"

"Got it," said Paddy.

In the first two days of their training course, Gus and Paddy — alternating as pilots — made eight daylight trips and three night-time sorties.

The two men chatted over breakfast on the third day.

"That chap Gordon Cummins was executed yesterday," said Paddy.

"Who?"

"You know, the Blackout Ripper. Hanged by Pierrepoint at Wandsworth Prison. During an air raid, too."

"Oh yes, I remember. Do they know how many women he killed?" asked Gus.

"Four for sure, and two attempted murders. Terrible business."

"Yes," agreed Gus.

"I say, is it about time for us to try reducing the landing, do you think?" asked Paddy.

"Suppose so. Do you want to try it first, or shall I?"

"Given your, er, robust style with landings, Bouncer, I think I'll go first. Double-check the undercarriage — make sure that both green lights are glowing."

"Wilco!"

"What are we going to say to Flying Officer Bridges?" asked Paddy. "We can't mention the SOE. It's a court martial for anyone who breaths a word about the ops."

"We'll just have to lie. It doesn't matter what we say. We're going to get into a spot of bother whatever story we come up with. Let's pretend we've a wager on which of us can put the kite down in the shortest distance. What do you say?"

"Why pretend? I'll bet you a crate of beer I can get her down in a shorter distance than you can."

"Done," said Gus with a grin, and they shook on it.

Landing a Hudson called for a much larger circuit pattern than in a Lysander. It weighed about three times as much as a Lizzie and the approach needed to be at least ten knots faster. The two pilots agreed that the Hudson wasn't nearly so manoeuvrable as a Lizzie at slow speeds, and lining up for the final approach was by no means easy.

"Ready to land her?" asked Bridges.

"Roger," answered Paddy and he came round to port, reducing speed as he did so. The pilot's notes indicated that a safe landing speed was no slower than seventy-five knots. Paddy slowed to sixty-five.

"Too slow!" called Bridges. "You're going too bloody slow!"

Paddy ignored him and slowed to sixty knots.

"You're going to miss the bloody strip!" shouted Bridges.

"Oh bugger! So I am," said Paddy as he quickly opened up the throttle to full. The nine-cylinder Wright radial engines roared and the Hudson began to climb.

"Sorry, chaps," said Paddy. "Let's have another go."

"Sorry? You'll have us all killed. Now, don't let the speed drop below seventy-five knots!" shouted Bridges.

Ignoring protestations from the instructor, who had broken into a sweat, Paddy took the Hudson around onto another approach. Flaps partly down, Gus glanced at the air speed indicator. Seventy-five, seventy, sixty-five. Paddy cut the throttle just before the plane touched down. He immediately dropped the flaps fully down and applied the brakes firmly. The Hudson shuddered and came to a halt. Gus judged the distance from touchdown to a halt at five hundred yards.

"What the blinking heck are you up to?" bawled Bridges.

"We've a little bet on who can land in the shortest distance," admitted Gus. "Come on, Paddy, out you get. I want a go!"

Paddy O'Brian, a look of relief on his face, swapped seats with Gus, who taxied the Hudson to the end of the runway, pointed her nose into wind and took off. Ignoring both the shouting Bridges and the ultra-safe advice in the pilot's notes, Gus came into land even slower than Paddy had dared. With the flaps half down, he slowed the Hudson to just sixty knots, then cut the engines to tick over as the Hudson cleared a hedge at the end of the runway. As the wheels touched the ground, Gus dropped the flaps fully and slammed the brakes on hard, causing a massive screech as one of the wheels locked up and skidded along the runway. They shuddered to a halt.

"Four hundred bloody yards!" shouted Paddy, a broad grin on his face. "Beers are on me, Bouncer! Will you join us, Flying Officer Bridges?"

"Join you? I'll have you both bloody grounded!" shouted the furious instructor.

The course lasted just under a week, with Gus and Paddy both passing.

Back at Tempsford, the two men spent another week practising landing the Hudsons. Time and effort proved fruitful, and they eventually got the final approach speed down to fifty-five knots without stalling or dropping a wing. Approaching at that speed, they found it was possible to land the Hudson in three hundred and fifty yards, good enough for any SOE operations. On their advice, the rear gun turret on some of the Hudsons was taken out and extra ballast placed in the rear of the airframe to re-balance it. This adaptation massively improved the low-speed handling of the aeroplane. Then they began training the other pilots.

"Here comes trouble," said Gus gloomily one Wednesday morning, a few weeks after the course at Silloth.

A gleaming, jet-black, ten horsepower Hillman Minx drove through the gates at RAF Tempsford. A WAAF was in the driver's seat. Gus, meanwhile, was looking at the passenger. It was Grindlethorpe.

"Flight Lieutenant Beaumont, just the man I'm looking for," said Grindlethorpe, as he got out of the car. He looked at Paddy. "Are you O'Brian?"

"This is indeed Flight Lieutenant O'Brian," said Gus, officiously.

"I want you both in the squadron leader's office in ten minutes. Understood?"

"We're just off to brief some new pilots, actually. But we'll be with you in half an hour. Come on Paddy," said Gus. They walked away, leaving a speechless Grindlethorpe standing on the runway.

"Why did you tell him that? He's bound to check up on us," Paddy protested.

"No, he won't. We'll make him wait."

"Who the bloody hell is he, anyway?"

"Squadron Leader Titus Grindlethorpe," said Gus, and he quickly explained much of the history between them. "He's a bad egg if ever there was one. Worst of all, Paddy, he killed a good friend of mine, Stewart Poore. He ordered some ack-ack guns to open up, knowing damned well that Poorly's Hurricane was in the line of fire."

"Why on earth would he do that?"

"He was trying to get me. At least, I think he was. Leave the talking to me, Paddy. Chances are it's me he wants — he has nothing against you. But we'll soon find out. Come on."

The two pilots knocked on the squadron leader's office door and then entered when bid.

Grindlethorpe was at the desk, papers in his hands. They saluted.

"I have a report here from Flying Officer Bridges, and I have to say it's pretty damning. Anything to say for yourselves?"

"We..."

Gus kicked Paddy's foot. "We haven't seen the report, Squadron Leader, so we are hardly in a position to say anything. Let me have a look, would you?"

Grindlethorpe passed the report to Gus, who read it quickly then gave it to Paddy.

"We had to make up some excuse, didn't we? You know full well we can't tell anyone what we're up to," said Gus.

Paddy handed the report back to Grindlethorpe, but stayed silent.

"Flying Officer Bridges reports that the two of you made a bet with each other; a crate of beer to whoever landed the aircraft in the shortest distance. Is that true?"

"Yes, but it was just to throw him off the scent," said Gus.

"And he says he saw you, O'Brian, give a crate of beer to Beaumont. You were then both drinking beers from the crate later that afternoon."

"Well, that's true.."

"Then why did O'Brian give you a crate of beers?"

"Because Flight Lieutenant O'Brian is a thoroughly decent chap who appreciates my superior piloting technique and simply wanted to reward me. Isn't that right, Flight Lieutenant O'Brian?"

"Absolutely spot on! Flight Lieutenant Beaumont is a terribly good pilot, Squadron Leader. I especially like his soft landings. Sublime!"

"And that's the story you're going to stick with, is it, Beaumont?"

"It's the truth, Squadron Leader. The whole truth and nothing but the truth," said Gus, removing his cap to smooth down his hair.

"Have I given you permission to remove your headgear, Beaumont?"

Gus straightened his shoulders, folding his forage cap under his left epaulette. "No, I don't believe you did, Squadron Leader, but it's a little stuffy in here. Must be all the hot air."

"I'll have you for insubordination if you're not careful, Beaumont! Now get out, both of you. Go, before I change my mind."

Gus turned without saluting and walked out of the room. Paddy, with just the faintest suggestion of a salute, followed close behind him.

PART TWO: A DOUBLE IN THE CELL

CHAPTER 23

Gus flew the Hudson down from Tempsford to Tangmere in the morning. Once he'd landed, he taxied the aircraft to the side of the base where the cottage was situated and parked up. The ground crew quickly busied themselves refuelling and checking the Hudson over as he, Paddy O'Brian and the new Flight Sergeant, Edward Burns sauntered to the cottage.

"What's that?" asked Gus, looking down at Paddy's boots.

"It's a knife, of course. I always carry one on moonlight drops. You never know when it might come in handy, Gus."

After a cup of tea, the three airmen climbed back into the Hudson at midnight. Full moon was at 21:13, ideal for a night flight. Paddy took the controls on the port side of the large, Perspex-encased cockpit. Gus, armed with a map, compass and pencil, strapped himself into the seat to Paddy's right and just behind him. Flight Sergeant Burns carried two flasks of coffee and a basket of sandwiches. "The Joes will need these," he said as he took up his position in the fuselage of the aeroplane.

"Save some for us, Burnie. We'll have it on the return leg," called Paddy.

Then the passengers arrived, two men and a woman, all in civvies and carrying small cases. Gus immediately recognised Eunice and Duncan. *Bloody hell*, he thought. *Who's set this up? Peacock or Grindlethorpe?* There was no point making a fuss. He didn't even let on to Paddy that he knew two of the Joes.

Burns settled the agents into the seats at the back of the Hudson. Soon they were airborne, soaring over the sky above Sussex, heading for the sea. Gus looked down as they crossed the French coast, bathed in moonlight. No flak. Good. The

Hudson banked as Paddy turned to port and took up a new course.

"On course for the landing zone," he said. "ETA twenty-five minutes."

This was the most dangerous part of any mission — flying over German-occupied France, not knowing if there were any Ju-88 or Bf-110 night fighters out hunting. The flight hadn't lost any kites to enemy fighters, but there was always a first time.

"Five minutes. Keep your eyes peeled," called Paddy.

"Landing strip is right ahead of us. See anything?"

"Nothing," said Flight Sergeant Burns.

"We're right on top of it," said Gus. "No flares. Nothing! Bloody agents are late."

"I'll go around for another run."

Paddy opened up the throttles and the twin Wright Cyclone radial engines roared. He turned the Hudson to starboard and began to gain height. Suddenly, a searchlight flooded the sky, the glare dazzling the crew of the Hudson.

"Bugger!" yelled Paddy. "It's a bloody trap!"

The Hudson twisted and turned, weaving a violently irregular course through the night sky as Paddy tried to escape the powerful beam of light. But the Germans were well-trained and good at their jobs. They manoeuvred the light, keeping the meandering Hudson in their beam. Then the German ack-ack gun opened up. Two Flakvierling 38 anti-aircraft quads, a total of eight gun barrels, had been perfectly positioned to trap the plane in a crossfire as it turned at low altitude. Gus caught a glimpse of the two gun crews working frantically, but with a slick, well-practised routine, changing the twenty-round magazines on each gun every six seconds.

The Hudson shuddered under the impact of those twenty-millimetre shells, which ripped into it at close range.

"Paddy, are you all right?" shouted Gus.

He mopped the sweat from his brow and felt his heart beating fast. There was no response. Through the smoke that began to fill the cockpit, Gus looked at his friend slumped over the joystick, blood oozing from a wound to his head.

"Burnie, help me get him out!" shouted Gus, but as he glanced behind him into the body of the aeroplane, he saw that the flight sergeant was lying motionless on the floor. Gus shouted through to the back of the Hudson: "Duncan, get up here quick! I need help. The pilot's strap's jammed. You'll find a knife tucked into Paddy's left boot. Cut him out!"

Between them, Duncan and Gus managed to pull Paddy's body from the seat and Gus took the controls. Flames were streaming from the port engine; altitude was three hundred feet. He turned the Hudson away from the anti-aircraft guns and tried to gain height. Then he saw a field in the moonlight, pushed the joystick and flew towards it. Out of range of the guns and clear of the searchlight, Gus struggled to keep the Hudson level as he guided it towards the field. He had a vision of a beach in Corfu, crystal-clear water leading to white sand, with Cypress pines in the background.

"Is he alive, Duncan?"

"Sorry, no, he's gone."

"What about the flight sergeant? Take a look at him for me."

Duncan went to the rear of the Hudson's large cockpit. "He's dead, too."

"Eunice and the other chap in the back?"

"They're fine."

"Go back and get the rear door open, Duncan. Tell them to be ready to parachute out. I'm going to crash-land, and I don't want anyone near the kite when it comes down. We've got a lot of fuel on board. Jump as soon as you think you're low enough and get the hell out of the way."

"Roger, Gus. See you down there. Good luck."

Duncan scrambled back and Gus was aware of a flurry of activity, then the rush of air as the rear door opened. He guided the wounded Hudson towards the field, cut the engines and glided her down. He glanced behind and caught a glimpse of Eunice fleeing the cabin. Then the crash of metal on ploughed land deafened him as the Hudson belly-flopped and dug into the field.

The Germans would already be pursuing him. Sweating and fighting for breath, Gus threw himself out of the cockpit, landing heavily on his ankle. Wincing, he looked up. A hundred yards away, clearly silhouetted against the moonlit sky, he saw a large copse. Checking that he had his pilot's escape pouch and Webley revolver, Gus rose and made his way as fast as he could towards the trees.

Only when he was well into the woods did Gus dare pause to catch his breath. He turned towards the ruined Hudson. Just as he did so, there was a loud whoosh. The petrol had caught fire.

Gus dropped to the ground and exhaled loudly. What to do next? The Jerries were sure to find him if he stayed here. They'd surround the copse and flush him out. If he made a run for it over open ground, he would be shot. Would he have to give himself up, and spend the rest of the war in a German POW camp?

CHAPTER 24

Suddenly, Gus heard a voice amidst the trees.

"*Monsieur.*" It was a woman's voice, little more than a whisper. "*Monsieur*, quickly, come this way. We have little time."

Saying nothing, she led Gus through the dense woodland. She set the pace, a cross between a quick march and scout's pace. They proceeded in single file along narrow paths. Gus noticed that she looked back regularly to check that he was keeping up. When they reached a gateway in a wider track at the end of the woods, she paused.

"*Parlez-vous Français, monsieur?*"

"*Oui*," he answered, "but please try not to speak too quickly."

She smiled, which helped him relax a little. "We're safe now," she said in French. "The Nazis can't get around this side of the woods easily. They won't try it at night. I see you are limping."

"Yes. I hurt my ankle in the crash."

"The bad news is that we have another three kilometres to go until we reach a safehouse. Do you think you can manage to walk that far? We can go more slowly now, and I can support you on one side if it helps."

Gus's ankle was hurting like hell and felt twice its normal size, but he forced a smile. "I'll be fine. Thanks anyway."

This time they walked side by side and chatted a little.

"I'm Gustaw — Gus. Thanks for the help just now," said Gus. "What happened?"

"One of our group was arrested by the police yesterday. They must have made him talk. As soon as we knew he'd been taken in, we tried to make contact to call off the drop. But it was too late. None of our people were inside the perimeter of the drop; we were scattered around, to be on hand if we could."

"What's your name? I mean, what do I call you?"

"Call me Monique."

"Are the others safe?"

"I don't know. I saw three fall from the aeroplane before you altered course. Hopefully they're in safe hands. I'll meet my comrades tomorrow and find out. What about your crew?"

"Dead. Both of them."

"I'm sorry. Hopefully we'll meet the agents tomorrow."

Monique, though Gus assumed that wasn't the woman's real name, led him through the still, moonlit night following a winding lane. Soon they stopped, climbed a fence and cut through a number of fields. Then Gus spotted a small farm in the distance with a solitary barn.

Ten minutes later, they were inside the barn. "You'll be safe here," said Monique.

"Where am I?"

"You are in one of the barns on the Deneuves' farm. The old farmer is a drunkard who never ventures out and his son, Claude, is one of us. He'll come with food tomorrow."

"You're a Resistance cell?"

"Yes. A small one."

"Have you been busy?"

"We do what we can. The other night, Claude and I were in Dieppe delivering leaflets. We killed two of *les doryphores*."

"Sorry, my French isn't up to that."

"*Les doryphores* are what we call the Nazis. You see, last winter was very harsh. Everyone kept their fires alight. The cold affected the occupying troops as much as us. They had a severe shortage of firewood, and they fuelled their stoves with anything that would burn. They chopped down private woodland, and German troops scoured the villas along the seafront for doors, window frames and parquet flooring. We locals are sure we lost more wood to the Nazis than we did to the outbreak of Colorado beetles last summer. So we began to call the occupying Germans *les doryphores*. Beetles."

"You said you killed a couple of them?"

"We saw them staggering out of one of the brothels in the port and decided to follow them. They were very drunk. When they got to the dock, it was easy to just push them into the water. Splash, splash — just like that!"

"Are you Gaullists or communists?"

"Does it matter?"

"Not really. I'm just interested."

"We're communists. We were all members of the local Communist Party before the German invasion. We're part of the Francs-tireurs et partisans Français — the FTP, but we work alongside the Gaullists. Marcel Prenant is the FTP's Chief of Staff; his main role is to act as liaison between us and the Gaullist resistance groups. Baudouin doesn't care much for this arrangement. He thinks the Gaullists are right-wing extremists, little better than the Nazis."

"Who's Baudouin?"

"He's our cell commander — but it's a codename, of course."

"He's a bit harsh, isn't he? The Gaullists don't kill Jews."

"If they take power after the war, they'll kill us. Baudouin thinks we shouldn't be co-operating with them. Who is de

Gaulle, anyway? Nobody knows anything about him. Maybe you English invented him." She laughed. "I'm exaggerating. We know he's real. His influence here in France is growing. It doesn't matter that few know anything about him. Those students in Paris were shouting '*Vive de Gaulle*' just as loudly as they shouted '*Vive la France*'. In Vichy, when Pétain talks about subversives and dissidents, he never mentions de Gaulle, but everyone knows who he means. But still, he's a conservative — he and his people will turn on us after the war."

"First we have to win the war," said Gus.

"Yes, and right now de Gaulle is the only French leader that is prepared to fight. Look, I have to go now. You'll be perfectly safe here tonight, so don't worry. Tomorrow, Claude will arrive with food. He'll announce himself with the password 'Jacobin' just to let you know he's a friend. No need to answer. Got that?"

"I understand."

"Goodnight, then."

"Goodnight, and thanks, Monique. Without your help, I'd be a POW by now."

Once she'd gone, Gus took off his flying boots and socks to examine his painful ankle. It was blue and swollen. *Better keep off my feet for a day or two if I can*, he thought. He looked at his wristwatch: 0500 hours, and an hour later for the French. It must be getting light outside. Claude would be early, he expected, being a farmer. Gus would try to get some sleep. As he settled himself, a cockerel began its morning efforts, and soon he heard the sound of cattle outside the barn.

CHAPTER 25

Gus had hardly dozed off before he heard footsteps and shouts. "Jacobin! Jacobin!" someone called.

The door of the barn swung slowly open, creaking on its hinges. A young man — Gus put him at sixteen or seventeen years of age — with a smouldering Gauloises dangling from his bottom lip, strolled into the barn. He was dressed in fawn-coloured flannels and a grubby white shirt with the sleeves rolled up. A black beret completed his distinctly rural outfit. A dog followed him in, some sort of gundog, thought Gus, judging by its long ears. It ambled over to him, its docked tail twitching furiously.

"Get back, Blue," said Claude.

"It's all right. I'm fine with dogs. What breed is he?"

"He's a Picardy Spaniel."

The dog was chocolate-brown with lighter, sandy-coloured markings. Gus felt the cold wetness of its nose as it nuzzled against his hand. Its squarely built, muscular body stood about two feet at the withers. Gus stroked the dog's coat, and it looked at him with vibrant amber eyes.

"You call him Blue?"

"Blue, yes. Because he's mostly brown." Claude laughed. "I've got some food for you, *monsieur*. Bread, butter, some coffee."

"Thanks. I'm hungry."

"I see from your uniform you're an airman. A pilot?"

"Yes."

"Have you ever flown in a Spitfire, *monsieur*?" asked Claude, his eyes wide.

144

"Yes, I have, as a matter of fact, but don't keep calling me *monsieur*. I'm Bouncer, Bouncer Beaumont."

The teenager offered his hand, which Gus accepted and shook. "Claude Deneuve. Spitfires are the best fighters, yes?"

"Yes, they're pretty damned good," smiled Gus.

"Here, *Monsieur* Bouncer. Take the food, eat. Would you like a cigarette?"

"Not for me, thanks."

Gus poured some coffee and spread butter onto the white bread. It tasted delicious. Claude sat down, took another Gauloises from the packet and lit it. The foul smell forced Blue to retreat to the doorway.

"The woman, Monique, said three people were seen falling from my aeroplane," said Gus. "She thought they might have been picked up by your comrades."

"I hope so, but I don't know. We'll just have to wait. Did you fly in the Battle of Britain?"

"Yes. I flew Hurricanes. Monique said it's just you and your father at the farm?"

"That's right. My elder brother Jacques was an infantry reservist. He was killed in May 1940 holding up the German tanks while the British ran back home. Oh, sorry…"

"No need. We all know Dunkirk was a mess."

"Then the Germans took Gerrard, my other brother, for war work in Germany. Look, I have to get back to work. I think Monique will be back this evening, and maybe our leader. If they have found your friends, they'll bring them along, but not until dusk. I'll come back with more food this afternoon. Goodbye for now, *Monsieur* Bouncer."

The pleasant summer weather helped Gus to rest and recuperate. He'd ventured outside to wash himself by the river and discovered that, even in daylight, the small farm felt totally isolated. This particular barn was more secluded than the rest of the buildings. Gus took off his uniform jacket and folded it into a pillow. Then he removed his shirt and lay down to rest in the hot afternoon sun. After a while he was disturbed by something furry by his head. Blue had joined him.

As evening settled over the farm, it became a little cooler. Gus dressed and moved back to the barn. As the light began to fade, he heard footsteps outside, then Monique appeared. She was quickly followed by Eunice, her arm in a sling, Duncan, the boy Claude, and another, older man Gus didn't recognise.

Eunice rushed towards him. Gus smiled and opened his arms, and she flung herself into them.

"It's nice to see you too," he whispered, hugging her close, "but you've just dropped your cover, my dear."

"I don't bloody care," she blurted. "I thought you'd died in that plane crash."

"Did you hurt your arm in the landing?"

"Yes. It's not broken, just badly sprained."

Gus broke free from her embrace and looked at the others. Duncan shook him by the hand. "Well done, old boy. I have to confess I was a tad worried for a time last night. Never did like aeroplanes — that's why I joined the Ox and Bucks. Let me introduce Baudouin." Duncan waved towards the older man. "He's the leader of the cell."

With Claude and Monique, the six of them sat in a tight circle in the barn, their voices low. Apart from the occasional rustling of the straw, the barn was silent.

"How did you get away?" asked Gus.

"We were lucky," said Duncan. "We had soft landings well away from where the Jerries were surrounding the landing zone. One of Baudouin's men came up quickly and led us to safety. We spent the night in somebody's attic, all three of us.

These two came round this morning." He waved towards Baudouin and Monique.

"What about the other man?"

"The wireless operator is fine. He checked the kit and nothing's broken. They've moved him somewhere else now."

"We have important things to discuss," Baudouin interrupted. "Your father doesn't know we're here, does he, Claude?"

"He knows nothing. He's in a drunken stupor as usual."

"As you know," said Baudouin to all assembled, "we have very bad news, I'm afraid. One of our men has been arrested by the *gendarmes*. We must presume they have by now handed him over to the Nazis, but we don't know that for sure. If he's been handed over, the bastards will have made him talk. Perhaps that's how they knew about the drop last night."

"You think that's what happened?"

"To be honest, I don't know. I can't see how Louis — he's the one that's been taken in — had details of it. He wasn't involved — he's too old for that sort of work."

"What does he do?" asked Gus.

"He's a schoolteacher and amateur painter. He goes outside, sits and sketches. Then he paints."

A brooding silence swept over the group.

"You," said Baudouin, pointing to Gus. "We'll have to keep you here at the farm. Claude will take care of you." He turned to Duncan. "You can go to Resistance HQ in Rouen tomorrow as planned. Monique will take you. But not you." He turned to Eunice. "That arm and sling makes you too conspicuous. You can pass as French. We'll be totally open about your presence in Dieppe. I'll pass you off as a family friend."

"What? In your own house? Are you sure that's safe?" asked Monique.

"What could be safer?" asked Baudouin. "I'll hide her right under Nussbaum's nose."

"Who is Nussbaum?" asked Gus.

"Kriminaldirektor Günther Nussbaum is the head of the Gestapo in the Dieppe area. He's been billeted in Baudouin's house," said Monique.

"So, you'll just have to sit it out here, Gus," said Eunice. "Monique will take Duncan to Rouen. When she's back, we can assess the situation. We'll have to think about getting back to England, if the cell has been uncovered."

"And just how do you propose we do that?" asked Gus.

"We can get the operator to send a message to London on the wireless. We'll ask for a Lysander to come in on the next full moon," replied Eunice.

"But, there's nowhere safe around here for a landing. Not now."

"We can find another landing site, kilometres away from here," said Baudouin.

"Well, let's get onto that as soon as we can," said Eunice. "Baudouin, please can you go to Maurice and have him report to London straight away. Tell him we need a pick-up organising as soon as possible. We'll get Gus out at the same time, if possible."

"Yes, leave it to me," said Baudouin.

"When is the next full moon?" asked Monique.

"Let's work it out," said Gus, pausing to undertake a little mental arithmetic. "It was the twenty-seventh of July yesterday, so … so it will be the night of the twenty-fifth of August — the full moon will appear very early in the morning on the twenty-sixth."

"Four weeks!" Monique exclaimed.

There were frowns all around. With that, Gus's visitors rose and left him alone. He was pleased they'd come, and impressed that Eunice had taken charge of the situation. He still felt a residual warmth from her embrace.

CHAPTER 26

"Tell me about flying a Spitfire, *Monsieur* Bouncer," said Claude the following day, when he brought Gus his food. "Tell me what is like fighting the Nazis in the air."

Gus relented and told the boy what he wanted to know. He talked about the outbreak of war and how he'd attacked a German armoured patrol in a Westland Lysander. Then he told him about the Defiant night fighters, single-engined planes armed with a four-gun turret. He described the Polish squadron in their Hurricanes and his short posting with 421 Flight's Spitfires. The boy was captivated, and Blue the spaniel lay by their feet, sleeping. In return, Gus was able to piece together something of Claude's life on the farm.

"Have you lived here long?"

"All my life. Ours is the only farm on the banks of the river Arques. It's a small farm, and the house is the only brick building on it. But it's home."

"How far from Dieppe are we?"

"Just a few kilometres south."

"And your father — tell me more about him, Claude."

"I remember one day — it was winter and I'd been out in the fields all morning. At that time of year, there's plenty of kale and roots, such as turnips and celeriac. The problem was that the earth was frozen and would not give, so I struggled to push the garden fork into it. I tried to put my weight on it and rock to and fro, but the ground still wouldn't yield. All that happened was that the prongs bent. I was tired and frustrated so, with my fork over my shoulder and Blue obediently following, I trudged back from the fields to the house. When I got there, I found the front door ajar, letting out what little heat issued from the smoky old stove in our kitchen. I stepped inside and shouted for Papa. We needed to keep the door closed to conserve heat. 'There's not much firewood left in the store!' I shouted at him. There was no answer.

"I looked around the kitchen. A packet of Gauloises and an envelope, both open, had been left on the table. Beside them was an empty coffee cup and half a bottle of Calvados. The old fool was drunk again! I asked myself, why did I have to do all the work on my own? I picked up the envelope and examined the postmark. It was a letter from Germany. I helped myself to a glass of cider from Papa's store, lit one of the cigarettes and sat down. I removed the piece of paper from the envelope and began reading it. It was a letter from Gerrard, my elder brother — he'd been conscripted by the Nazis. Those bastards had ruined everything. My father had fought them in the 1914 war, you see, and whatever he'd witnessed drove him to drink. My brother Jacques, a reservist, was killed in May 1940. And now the Nazis had taken Gerrard.

"I went to the larder, where I found a baguette and the remains of a wheel of Camembert. I picked up the bread knife, chopped the baguette in two and smothered half of the cheese onto it. Then I poured a drop of Calvados into an empty glass, and in one gulp I downed it. It made me cough."

"So, you're the man of the house?"

"In a way, yes. It felt like that at the time. I pulled on a thick coat and went outside for more wood. Then I checked on the few animals we kept. The two cows seemed content in the barn; I'd have to return later to milk them. The pig rootled around the yard, oblivious to the fact that it would be slaughtered in a few days' time to provide pork for Christmas, as well as sausages and pudding that last us into spring. Most of the chickens had retreated into their coop, and Blue rounded up the last few stragglers.

"Back at the house, I went to the gun cabinet and took out a shotgun and half a dozen cartridges. 'Come on, Blue, we're going hunting,' I said. The dog's ears pricked up and we marched off into the woods. I'll never forget that day. I think it's the day I became a man."

Claude told Gus more about the farm and the area. The Deneuves' small farm was totally dependent on the local agricultural co-operative. His great-grandfather, Maurice Deneuve, had been a founding member of this co-op many years before. He'd ensured that it linked to Dieppe's trade union activists and that its aims were rooted in improving working conditions and achieving fairer distribution of wealth. This was how the Deneuves had become bound up with local socialism and the Communist Party. Claude yearned for those days again — since the invasion and occupation, it was difficult to earn enough to keep him and his father. Any extra francs were a bonus. So Claude regularly travelled by bicycle into Dieppe, supplying produce to selected brassieres and restaurants, one of which was the Tout Va Bien where Monique worked as a waitress.

He also often went hunting with the spaniel. Claude and Blue hunted for partridges in and around the crop fields from late September to November. Pheasants were to be found in the woods from early November through to January. They would also take mallards, woodcocks, woodpigeons and rabbits whenever the opportunity arose.

"He's a good gundog, then," said Gus, looking at Blue.

"Yes. I trained him, with *Monsieur* Outhier's help. He's a neighbour. After my mother died, he took me under his wing and taught me to shoot. My father was never interested."

"Where does he live?"

"About two kilometres away. He lives in a grand, two-storey house surrounded by neat, well-kept grounds. That's where we trained the gundogs, in those gardens. I'd throw a ball as far as possible, commanding the dog to stay. Then I'd order the dog to fetch, and he'd sprint after the ball. I used to say 'drop', but *Monsieur* Outhier corrected me. He told me that if the dog drops a wounded bird, it may fly away. He taught me to order the dogs to place prey into my hand. From the ball we progressed to dead birds. *Monsieur* Outhier, limping slowly ahead, would try to conceal the bird, then I'd encourage the dog to search it out and retrieve it. Eventually, we practised shooting with an air rifle, then a shotgun."

"Why does he limp?"

"He was wounded during the Great War. He told me it was a bad wound — he almost lost the leg."

"And are you a good shot?"

"*Monsieur* Outhier says I'm an excellent shot — as good as himself. I can bag a mallard in flight easy as anything, but I'd rather be aiming at Nazis."

CHAPTER 27

A few days later, Eunice and Baudouin returned to the barn. Baudouin had a handwritten document with him.

"It's the report, Gus," said Eunice. "Peacock told me and Duncan about it."

"What report?"

"On the defences around Dieppe…"

"You can fill him in on the background later," said Baudouin. "It's very detailed, based on observations made by Claude and Monique, and there are three copies of it. I compiled it by hand. Louis typed it, along with a carbon copy. Both typed copies are accompanied by detailed drawings made by Louis. It's far too long and comprehensive to be sent by wireless; the Germans would easily locate the sender and expose the cell."

"Can you read it to us, Eunice, translating into English as you go along?"

"I'll try." She held the paper in both hands and began. "*Overview: The enemy makes little use of Dieppe. It serves only as a base for patrol craft and minesweepers and is likely to be of importance only in the event of a German invasion of England.*

"*Since April last year, 302 Static Infantry Division has occupied the coastal area from Le Tréport in the east to Veules-les-Roses in the west. This division is untried in battle. It is commanded by Major-General Konrad Haase, who is both energetic and efficient. He keeps his troops on their toes. Haase's HQ is at Envermeu, fifteen kilometres south-east of the town. The Dieppe sector is manned by 571 Regiment under Oberstleutnant Hermann Bartelt.*

"Many of the original soldiers have been drafted to the Eastern Front. Their replacements are Poles, Czechs and Belgians. We have even heard what we think are Russians.

"Part one: Natural defences. The attached drawings illustrate the nature of the area around Dieppe, as well as the Dieppoise beaches. As can be seen, the area is difficult to attack and easy to defend. The cliffs around the town rise up to great heights. The few narrow ravines have been blocked with concrete, wire and, we believe, around fourteen thousand landmines.

"The beach in front of the town shelves steeply. The beach is made up of thick, smooth pebbles as broad and flat as tea plates. They have a tendency to slither underfoot. Furthermore, the tides tend to push these pebbles into a succession of undulating slopes up to a one-in-four gradient.

"Our people have watched the Germans undertake tank trials on these beaches. The pebbles proved impossible, and the armour had to be dragged up on winches. The Germans have laid no tank-traps — they are not needed. Disembarkation at Pourville, at the mouth of the River Scie, is inadvisable as the estuary has been deliberately flooded.

"Part two: Artillery defences. Numerous defensive positions, many camouflaged from aerial view, have been constructed along the cliffs by teams of Dutch and Belgian workers. A string of concrete bulwarks have been constructed along the coast.

"Two heavy gun batteries are positioned on either side of the town. At Berneval there are three 170mm and four 105mm guns; at Varengeville there is a battery of six 155mm guns.

"In a horseshoe around the town there is a perimeter of further, lighter weapons. Six 88mm guns on the eastern cliff-tops by the church of Notre-Dame-de-Bon-Secours. Inland from this are four French 105mm guns and a further six 155mms at Arques-la-Bataille.

"The big cliffs on the western side of Dieppe are home to six 88mms, four 105s and numerous 37mm and 20mm cannon. In the grounds of the old château are two 75mm guns and two heavy mortars.

"All of these artillery pieces have good, uninterrupted fields of vision across the beaches and sea, as many properties along the sea front have been demolished recently.

"Part three: Infantry defences. There are numerous, too many to count, 34mm machine-gun (MG) posts on the headlands and cliffs on each side of the beaches. These MGs can cover almost every centimetre of the beach. Below the western headland there are reinforced casements housing 75mm and 37mm guns and flamethrowers.

"The seafront has been turned into a bastion against frontal attack. There are sand-bagged firing positions for snipers and MGs in every building standing along the seafront. For example, the casino has been turned into a fortress, with MG and sniper positions on each floor and a 37mm gun at the entrance.

"Finally, the vigilance of the troops is determined by weather and tide conditions. If the wind is strong, units on the seafront are relaxed to level three. If there is dead calm when the moon and tide favour an attack, vigilance is raised to level one."

Eunice stopped reading and looked up.

"Once your high command reads the report," said Baudouin, "they'll turn their backs on a Dieppe raid. They'll never attack here. It would be suicidal."

"They shouldn't," said Claude. "Every one of us knows that Dieppe would be the most difficult part of the coast to attack."

"What became of the three copies of the report?" asked Eunice.

"One copy, the typed original, was picked up by a Lysander."

Eunice shot a worried glance at Gus. "When was that?"

"A month before you landed."

"Nothing got through to my HQ," said Eunice.

"Then the plane must have been shot down — or perhaps it crashed?"

Gus shook his head almost imperceptibly.

"The second copy?"

"The carbon copy. That was the back-up and it went by a less certain route. It was smuggled along the O'Leary route with some rescued airman — through France, into Spain and then on to Gibraltar. It should have been received in England by now."

"It hadn't been received at the time we left," said Eunice.

"Perhaps it was intercepted, but I think it got as far as the Spanish border, at least. I'll double-check that. There's still time, though."

"That leaves the third. The handwritten original that you have," said Eunice.

"Yes. The Allies only asked for two," said Baudouin. "Claude suggested we burn it, as it would incriminate everyone within spitting distance if the Nazis got their hands on it. I thought we should get it to the Allies ourselves. It's so important — they must see it. But how?"

"We'll take it with us when the next Lysander comes," said Eunice.

"That's still more than three weeks away."

Eunice frowned. "We can't wait that long."

"What do you want me to do?" asked Gus. "Pinch a German aeroplane and fly it over to Blighty tomorrow?"

"I just don't know."

Later, Gus and Eunice were sitting together in the barn. "Tell me more about the report," said Gus.

"Peacock and Grindlethorpe commissioned a detailed report on Dieppe's defences. We know the Resistance cell have been collecting information about the Dieppe beaches, but nothing has reached London. Grindlethorpe told me he'd concluded that one of the cell may be a double agent. Either that, or somehow the Germans are intercepting information from them and stopping it getting back to us. We need that intelligence, and we need to know where the weakness in the chain is."

Gus looked at Eunice. "And that's your job? To find out what happened to the report?"

"Yes."

"So, Peacock specifically requested this report and sent in a Lysander to pick it up. A kite with one of our agents aboard, or with intelligence of that magnitude, would be met by him or one of his men in London. So why doesn't he have the report? Something's not right."

"You're right. When Duncan and I were briefed, we were categorically assured that the report hadn't arrived. The plane must have crashed, Gus. There's no other explanation. And if they don't see the report, and decide to launch some sort of attack on Dieppe, it could be an absolute disaster."

"No," said Gus, shaking his head. "We haven't lost a Lizzie for months. We're a small, tight-knit group. If a pilot doesn't return from a sortie, we would know."

"Then either Sir Alex lied to us about the report arriving, or he didn't know about its arrival."

"There is another possibility."

"What's that?"

"The double agent is at our end, in London. Somebody is deliberately concealing information from Peacock. Who else might have met that Lysander?"

"Grindlethorpe."

"Titus bloody Grindlethorpe! His name keeps popping up, doesn't it? I want you to talk me through that briefing, Eunice. I want to know everything that was said."

"We were in Peacock's office in Baker Street. There were five of us: Peacock, Grindlethorpe, Duncan, me and the wireless operator, Maurice Montluc. That's not his real name, obviously. Peacock reminded us that some potential agents fall at the initial hurdle, the SOE's preliminary school. He told us these unfortunates were whisked away to what he called the 'cooler', never to be seen again by those who progress. Grindlethorpe encouraged Peacock to press on — I could see he was beginning to get bored. 'You three, have, of course, progressed,' Peacock said, waving towards me, Duncan and Maurice. 'In fact, you've done very well indeed. Miss Hesketh has graduated and done two tours of duty to France. And Mr Farquhar here came out as the best of his cohort in unarmed combat.'"

Gus considered his friend. Duncan wasn't a terribly big man; he stood at five feet nine inches without his shoes. But he was strong. At Oxford, he'd excelled at both rowing and rugby. He'd also done some boxing. The SOE training had hardened his muscles and rendered him fit. He also seemed confident, and so he should, thought Gus. Having bludgeoned that unsuspecting German sentry in order to steal his uniform proved that he wasn't squeamish.

"Carry on telling me about the briefing, Eunice."

"Where was I? Yes, well, the conversation turned to Duncan's lack of French. Duncan admitted that he'd always struggled to learn it. It wasn't the grammar or the new words, it was his accent, apparently. Appallingly bad, insisted his teacher. Peacock said it didn't matter that Duncan's French was poor. He'd never need to pass himself off as French — Peacock said that was why I was going with him. Duncan was then given a new identity. He was now Georges Sauveterre, with a French-style suit and beret. I laughed and said he couldn't even pronounce his own bloody name."

"Duncan will be fine, then, as long as he doesn't open his mouth," said Gus with a chuckle.

"Peacock said this was a special briefing, that this sortie was top secret. The purpose on the face of it was to support our French comrades, but Peacock also wanted to learn more about this particular Resistance setup in Normandy. The government are planning for when the war is over, you see. Once the war is finished, they'll need to know which side these particular Resistance fighters are on."

"Peacock wants to know if they're Reds," said Gus.

"That's right. He said that some of the French who are prepared to fight the Germans are Gaullists, whom he considers to be like us. But he fears there are others in the wider Resistance movement who would rather take France further to the left — socialists, communists and the like. He wants to know which side of the fence Baudouin and the Dieppe cell sit on. That's what the mission is all about, Gus."

"I see."

"Duncan bears the brunt of it. When he's at Resistance HQ in Rouen, he needs to somehow get a grasp of their political colours. Peacock insisted that the people there would speak good English. They think Duncan's there as an escape expert, but his job is to get to know them."

"They're communists."

"How do you know?"

"I asked Monique."

"That simple, was it?"

"Yes. She's got nothing to hide. What about you, Eunice? What did Peacock want you to do?"

"Peacock and Grindlethorpe were recently back from a Combined Operations meeting. What they picked up there was extremely worrying. The meeting was led by Jock Hughes-Hallett, Lord Mountbatten's naval adviser. You see, Combined Ops are looking to Dieppe for a future mission. Anyway, Hughes-Hallett told them that intelligence reports indicate Dieppe is not heavily defended. All of the beaches in the vicinity are suitable for landing infantry, and some are even suited to landing tanks."

"Tanks?" queried Gus.

"Yes. God only knows what they've got planned. Anyway, Peacock was handed some photos to look at. Do you know what they were?"

"No idea," said Gus.

"A small collection of holiday snaps and postcards. The group of officers around the table looked at the postcards. One of them asked if this was all they had to go on. Peacock had the same worry. It seems the SOE have commissioned a report from the French. He thought it was with Combined Ops. 'What about the report we asked for?' he said. Peacock seemed agitated, nervous. I hadn't seen him like that before.

"Anyway, Hughes-Hallett carried on. He said that in terms of gradient, surface and subsurface, Combined Ops think the Dieppe beaches are most suitable for heavy tanks — Churchills. He said he was absolutely sure the Jerries haven't fortified the cliffs around the beaches because the RAF have been flying regular photoreconnaissance over the area, and they've seen little heavy artillery. There are some 88mm ack-ack guns that could be used against our vessels, but that's all. He thought we could knock those out with precision bombing minutes before the raid itself.

"Peacock asked if there were any questions. I asked who else would be going in with Duncan, Maurice and I, but it was just us three. There were no more questions, so Grindlethorpe gave us the final briefing. He covered the flight first, telling us we'd go in the next night. No parachuting. A Hudson would land us — well, you know more than I do about the flight."

"Yes. Carry on."

"A map was pinned to a noticeboard. Grindlethorpe pointed to an area midway between Dieppe and Amiens, south of this village. Oisemont. The local Resistance would be there to meet us. He told us that the leader of the cell was codenamed Baudouin, and that was all we needed to know about him. Maurice would be radio-operator for the job; the Resistance would spirit him away and we wouldn't see him again until we were finished. Grindlethorpe said Baudouin and his people would keep Duncan and I safe for a few days, and then Duncan would be moved to Rouen to link up with Resistance top brass. I was to go too, as an interpreter.

"Once we were sure Duncan was among agents who spoke sufficiently good English, I was to head back to the cell near Dieppe. My objective would be to gather as much information as I could about German troop dispositions in and around Dieppe, especially along the coastline. All this intelligence was to go via Baudouin to Maurice, who would radio it through to London. At some stage, Duncan would tell the cell to send me back over to Rouen, and I would escort him back. At the end of the job, we were to rendezvous at the same drop zone. Grindlethorpe would send a kite, probably another Hudson, to get the three of us out. He asked if there were any questions. I asked who would decide when we had enough information. He said he would decide. He'd tell Maurice, as he'd be picking up all of his radio messages. Grindlethorpe would let him know if there were any gaps that needed filling.

"Duncan asked how he would get from Rouen to the cell. Grindlethorpe said we could leave that to the French; we could trust the Resistance there to do a good job. Maurice had been sitting there listening, puffing on a cigarette. Now he asked if the cell had been in action before. Grindlethorpe said they hadn't. 'How do we know if they're any bloody good, then?' asked Maurice. He said it was all very well for Grindlethorpe to stand there pontificating about how good these French agents were, but it was our lives he was risking. 'Good or not, they're all we have,' Peacock said. 'You'll just have to make the best of it. That's what we always do.' And I agreed with him."

"And that's it?" asked Gus.

"That's it."

"So Peacock was interested in whether or not the Resistance cell is communist or Gaullist, and it was Grindlethorpe who gave the detailed briefing. They were concerned about the Dieppe defences and this blasted report. Is that right?"

"Yes," said Eunice. "That's right."

CHAPTER 28

A week later Monique returned to the Dieppe area, having left Duncan in Rouen. She and Eunice visited the farm to bring some supplies for Gus. The three of them sat in the barn, Monique chatting to Eunice, Gus listening to their conversation.

"Tell me more about Nussbaum, will you?" said Eunice. "How do you know him?"

"I work in a café in town. The Tout Va Bien. It's a popular hangout for the Germans these days; there's nearly always a few off-duty soldiers in there. One of the women, Helene, left because of Günther Nussbaum. She had to leave. He got her pregnant then disowned her, of course. The locals know it's his child, but they blame her. Personally, I expect he forced himself on her."

"I see. He sounds bad."

"He is. To be honest, I don't really like working there, at the café. But I need to work, and occasionally I overhear things. Günther Nussbaum is a creature of habit; he pops in there most days. Everybody knows Nussbaum is Gestapo; Kriminaldirektor is his title. That's what Pierre, the manager, calls him. 'Herr Kriminaldirektor,' he'll say, 'your usual table, *monsieur*?' I always refer to him as the Fat Policeman."

"You were at work today?"

"Yes."

"And he was there?"

"Yes. He came in early in the morning. Pierre jumped up, dashed across the dining room and fussed over him. 'Herr Kriminaldirektor, your usual table?' he asked. '*Ja*. The usual,'

Nussbaum replied. He can hardly speak French. He handed Pierre his overcoat and hat, then leered at me with his awful, lecherous smile. I left it as long as possible, then walked over to him. He ordered ham, eggs and a cup of coffee. Then he shouted after me, 'And make sure the coffee is hot! Not like yesterday!'

"I looked towards Madame Escoffier, one of our regulars. As I walked towards the kitchen, I passed close to her and she tutted at Nussbaum. I think he heard — anyway, he scowled at her.

"I told Daniel — he's the under-chef — that the Fat Policeman wanted ham and eggs. I knew Daniel would have saved these precious items for the Gestapo man. He has to, you see. Nussbaum could make things very difficult for us at the café."

"It must be a hard war, living under occupation," said Eunice. "Do you live in Dieppe, Monique?"

"Yes. I rent a room in an old fishers' cottage in Le Pollet, the old part of town. It's the old fishing quarter on the eastern side of the port, where the painters used to flock before the last war."

"And the café work is all right?"

"The pay is poor. Look at these clothes." Monique looked down at her shabby dress and worn-out shoes. "Times are tough and money is scarce, but it's a job."

"How long did Nussbaum stay?"

"Less than an hour. That's usual. The Fat Policeman never comes in for lunch, thank God! He sometimes comes later in the day, though."

"Are you busy these days?"

"Lunchtime is usually busy, yes. The war makes it increasingly difficult to source some things; meat and eggs are scarce. But Daniel is a good cook and he can be innovative. The sea still provided its fruits. Today's menu was fish soup, followed by braised tripe with onions, always a favourite. Daniel had made a good *tarte tatin* to follow, though there was no cream. There's still plenty of cheap wine around the Dieppe bars and bistros, enjoyed by locals and off-duty Germans alike."

"Oh, I could murder a nice Kir Royale." Eunice and Gus both laughed. That had always been Eunice's drink of choice.

"We can't get champagne, but there's some nice crémant around, from Bourdeaux and Limoux. Anyway, in the afternoon Claude arrived from his father's farm. He stood his bicycle outside the Tout Va Bien and strode through the dining room and into the kitchen, carrying two bags of vegetables. Daniel asked him what he had this week. He said beans, beets and Swiss chard, as well as some tomatoes and onions. Back in the winter, Claude brought us a big bag of Jerusalem artichokes, which Daniel gratefully accepted.

"Pierre brought a young woman into the kitchen from the café. She's about the same age as Claude, maybe a year or two older. She was there for her induction; her name is Nicole. I looked at her bobbed, blonde hair and petite figure and immediately worried that she was bound to appeal to the Fat Policeman. I'd need to warn her."

"And did you?"

"Yes. She'd worked in a place on the other side of town. She asked if there were any difficult customers, so I told her about Nussbaum. 'Just don't talk to him more than you have to,' I said. She thanked me. I told her he'd been in already today and might return, but he rarely came after breakfast. The place is closed to locals at nine o'clock and we get a lot of soldiers coming in after that, once they've gone off duty. They're

166

mostly respectful, just lads and one or two older men. 'I'll be all right,' she said, and she told me not to worry."

"What did you do after work?"

"When I left the Tout Va Bien, I reached for a cigarette and lit it as I walked along the promenade behind the beach. I stopped at a small shelter and looked out to sea. The tide was out, and I looked towards the German gun positions, dug-in on the cliffs. A man wearing a brown tweed jacket and a dark maroon beret was there with his sketchpads. It was the teacher, Louis Lavigne. He's the one they arrested."

At this point, Gus interrupted. "He's back? But how did he survive?"

Monique shrugged. "I don't know yet, but you'll be able to ask him yourself. I'm sure you'll meet him soon."

CHAPTER 29

The next day, Baudouin, Claude and Monique came to the barn, this time accompanied by another man. He looked older than the rest and was dressed in tweed and a maroon beret. Gus guessed it was the schoolteacher, Louis Lavigne.

"I probably don't need to introduce Louis," said Baudouin. "As you can see, he's been released."

"Did they interrogate you?" asked Eunice.

"Yes. But all they wanted to know was why I painted out there in all weathers."

"What did you say? How did you convince them to let you go?"

"I told God's honest truth," said Louis.

"And what was that?"

"That I'm a frustrated artist, and I never wanted to be a schoolteacher," laughed Louis. "I explained that I taught the oldest of the junior-aged children in the small elementary school in Hautot-sur-Mer, which they knew anyway. I told them I'd had a bad week; I'd been off-colour and some of the boys were playing up. So on Sunday I took my small easel and paints to the beach. Since the war it's been difficult to get manufactured shades, so I mix my own greys. That Sunday I decided to use cool primaries to reflect the dullness of the Channel before me — cerulean blue, lemon yellow and alizarin crimson. I used an old rigger brush and a one-and-a-half-centimetre Hake brush, which I'd made myself years ago. The Hake had a raw, wooden handle and fine goat-hair bristles bound and glued into a split in the wood..."

"Hold on," said Eunice. "You said all of this to the Gestapo?"

"No, it wasn't the Gestapo. It was the local police."

"Let him continue," said Baudouin.

"They asked me why I was always painting on the beaches and cliffs. I told them that the Impressionists and Post-Impressionists had loved painting the coast and sea near Dieppe. Lebourg, Loiseau, Walter Sickert — they had all contributed. Claude Monet, the master himself, had created many paintings of Pourville and Dieppe. And now, I told them, it was my turn."

"They didn't say anything about you gathering detailed information?"

"They wondered why I often returned to the exact same parts of the beach."

"They've been watching you."

"Yes, of course. I told them I was more interested in the detail. That I scrutinised the beach, where, at low tide, the sand was exposed. Some large rocks jutted out here and there, as though trying to escape the sands. The higher part of the beach, closer to the highwater mark, was pebbles. The gradient, of course, varied at different points along the beach from Berneval, to the east of Dieppe, and Quiberville to the west. I said that by sketching and painting this length of coastline at various stages of the tide, I was able to detail all of these characteristics. In fact, I've done this so many times that I think I could draw the beaches from memory.

"They wanted to see some of my finished works. I said they could come back to my place and have a look. So, they did. I explained to them that I sketched in the field, took the roughs back to the small room on the upper floor of my house in the city, and painted there. The light was best in the early morning until about eleven o'clock. When a painting was finished, I told them I'd revisit the original scene and check it again. I showed them some of my finished work, as they asked."

"What did they say?"

"One of the policemen asked if he could buy one, for his wife's birthday present. He gave me ten francs for a seascape."

"Louis," said Baudouin, "you are a master. I think you've charmed them away from any and all suspicion they might have had."

"Or bored them half to death," said Claude with a boyish smile.

"I know you don't mean it," smiled the old teacher.

"I don't like it," said Gus a little later, when he and Eunice were alone. "I don't like it all."

"Why not?"

"If Louis didn't give them any information, then how did the Germans know we were going to land in that field? Could he be lying?"

"Possibly, but the others seem convinced."

"A different cell member, then?" suggested Gus.

Eunice was now jotting all of this down. "Or the Gestapo boss, Nussbaum — he might have pieced together more than anyone realised. Or he may have been lucky."

"It seems like they knew the landing zone but not much else. Neither the French police nor the local Gestapo have taken in any of the others. They haven't come snooping around here, or around Baudouin's place, have they?"

"No. Nussbaum is there now and again, but that's it."

"Let's assume, just for a moment, that the two are totally disconnected. Let's say that the Germans' knowledge of the drop and the arrest of the old man are simply a coincidence."

"Go on."

"That suggests any leak of information — assuming the leak isn't in London — is coming from higher up the chain than this small cell. Maybe it's a traitor in Rouen. When is Duncan due back, by the way?"

"Any day now. Monique's not going over there. Baudouin thinks it's too dangerous. An undercover agent will bring him."

PART THREE: OPERATION JUBILEE

CHAPTER 30

A few days later, Gus and Claude were having breakfast at the farm, with Blue enjoying a few scraps. Suddenly, Claude looked up.

"Listen, *Monsieur* Bouncer," he said with alarm. "A car engine."

Gus ran for cover in the barn as a car raced into the courtyard, tyres screeching as it came to a halt. Baudouin was at the wheel, with Eunice beside him. They got out and ran over to the barn.

"Monique was arrested by the police this morning," Eunice said in a rush. "And the police have rearrested Louis. Baudouin thinks they may have already handed them over to the Gestapo. Duncan will be devastated."

"It's a disaster. They'll talk," said Baudouin. "The Gestapo have ways of making people talk — methods you cannot imagine. We need to get out of here tonight."

"And go where?" asked Gus.

"To a safehouse for now, while we think of something. Maybe we can arrange another pick-up. It's not too far away — a small place called Vasterival, just a few kilometres west of Dieppe. We have a car. Get yourself ready; there's no time to lose."

"Wait," said Gus. "What about Duncan and the wireless operator — Maurice?"

"Maurice is safe. Neither Monique nor Louis know where he is. Duncan is on his way back from Rouen as we speak."

"He'll be brought here, though?"

"Yes. Claude can wait for him," said Baudouin. "He knows the way to Vasterival. The rest of us need to move, now. There's only two hours of darkness left."

"Let's get going, then," said Gus. "Eunice, have you brought your things?"

"Yes, they're in the car."

"And I've got mine," said Baudouin.

Gus didn't have much to get together. Claude had given him a pair of his father's boots, and he had the standard pilot's escape kit. He stuffed the French banknotes into his pocket with the compass, which he thought might come in useful. He also carried his Webley revolver.

"Let's go," he said.

The village of Vasterival was dominated by the Hôtel de la Terrasse, with its manicured lawns and tennis court. All around the hotel were villas and houses open in the season for visitors. One such villa was La Lézardière, a fine nineteenth-century house.

Opposite La Lézardière was a smaller but equally lovely holiday house, La Maisonnette. In its garden was a *pigeonnier*, of no practical use these days but regarded quaint by holidaymakers. Beneath the *pigeonnier* was a cellar that contained stores and hid Baudouin, Eunice and Gus. They had been holed up there for three days.

They'd travelled to Vasterival in the Citroën, going slowly, careful not to wake anyone. They drove without headlights, avoiding German patrols. Though they were all tense, the journey went without a hitch. Gus noticed the airfield at St Aubin as they drove by. "What do they use that for?" he asked.

"Nothing," said Baudouin. "It's just a small aerodrome. No bombers or fighters. A few communication aircraft, that's all."

The car was left discreetly in the fields behind Vasterival.

"We continue on foot," said Baudouin. "Bring your things."

Gus pushed his revolver into his pocket and grabbed Eunice's small bag. In the early dawn light the group felt exposed, but under Baudouin's guidance they soon reached the building they were looking for.

They were grateful for the cellar's security once they arrived. There was food and drink, and, over the next couple of days, they put in place a shift system, taking it in turns to keep a look out.

On the second morning, when Baudouin was on lookout duty, Gus turned to Eunice. "The other day, you said Duncan will be devastated when he finds out Monique has been captured."

"That's right."

"There was something between them?"

"Yes. You know Monique went to Rouen with him as his guide. She was also his safety-net, and often a bond forms between people in that situation. After she came back, she confided in me, saying they'd hit it off. To be honest, it sounded as though they'd fallen in love."

"Love? And what do you know about love, Eunice?" teased Gus.

"Oh, I know. I wasn't sure before, but I am now."

"Sure about what?"

"I'm sure that I love you, Gus."

He looked at her, taken aback. It was the last thing he'd expected Eunice to say. And now, of all times. He saw tears forming in her eyes and smiled, taking her hand. "I love you too, Eunice."

They kissed, a long, passionate kiss that atoned for months of missed opportunities. Then Eunice rested her head on Gus's shoulder. "But how will we ever get out of here?"

Gus glanced at his uniform. "If the police or Gestapo find me here with you, it will put everyone in a very dangerous position. I suppose I could hand myself over to the army; they won't mistreat a British officer and…"

"We're already in a dangerous position. The Gestapo will torture Louis and Monique. They'll break," said Eunice. "Maybe they have already."

"They don't know we're here. They might spill the beans about Duncan, though."

"I'm worried," said Eunice. "Let's hope he gets away before they do."

Darkness had fallen when they heard the agreed knock on the door. Baudouin went up to answer. It was Claude, and Duncan was with him.

Duncan hobbled painfully down the stone steps into the cellar, helped by the boy.

"Bloody leg's broken," said Duncan.

He sat down, twisting uncomfortably in a chair. "I just can't believe it," he said. "I've been captured by the Jerries, escaped from the Jerries, trained up as a Joe and parachuted into France only to be foiled by a bloody broken leg in a cycling accident! I can't walk on it — it's bloody murder!"

"We'll get you a doctor," said Baudouin. "I'll send for one tomorrow."

"You met with the Resistance in Rouen?" asked Eunice.

"Yes."

"Was Chevreuse there?"

"Yes, he was." Duncan looked at Gus. "Chevreuse is the codename for Professor Bloch."

"Marc Bloch? Is he well?" asked Gus.

"Yes," said Duncan. "Where's Monique?"

Eunice hesitated. "She's…"

"The Nazis have her," said Baudouin.

"Oh my God! They'll torture her. They'll…" Duncan struggled up, but the pain in his leg sent him reeling back into the chair.

CHAPTER 31

They were awoken in the dead of night by gunfire, shouts and the sound of aeroplane engines overhead. The owner of the house, Gaston Cadot, brought his wife Marie and young son, Gérard, down to the cellar beneath the *pigeonnier*.

"What's going on up there?" asked Claude.

"God only knows," said Gaston. "English ships are on the water, soldiers in the lanes and fields. The ground's littered with empty cartridges. Look —" he pointed to Gérard — "he burnt his fingers trying to pick one up."

"Do you mean British soldiers?" asked Eunice.

"Yes. And Germans."

"It's the invasion! We're saved," said Claude.

"No." Gaston reached into his pocket for the leaflet a British commando had given him and handed it to Eunice, who read it quickly.

"It's a raid," she said.

"A raid? Why a raid, here at Dieppe? We told the English fools how well prepared the Germans are here," said Gaston.

"It didn't get through," said Baudouin.

"Or it was intercepted," said Gus.

"By who?" asked Duncan.

"We don't know," said Eunice, "but apart from Peacock himself, Squadron Leader Grindlethorpe is the only one who we know had the opportunity."

Gus knew Grindlethorpe didn't like him, but surely he was a patriot. Surely he would have passed the report on Dieppe's defences to the SOE, wouldn't he?

Duncan shook his head slowly. Then he smiled. "At least a raid gives us a chance to escape," he said.

"How?"

Gus jumped to his feet. "Duncan's right," he said. "Invaders push on into the place they've invaded, but raiders return. Those soldiers are going back to England. They've come by air or sea, but their only way home is by boat, and we're going with them!"

"What do you suggest?"

"We go out now and make contact with the soldiers. Come on, get your shoes on."

"We can't take Duncan," said Baudouin. "The pathways to the beaches from here are steep and slippery. He won't make it with that leg."

"I'm not leaving him," said Eunice.

"Don't be silly," said Duncan. "I'll be fine."

"Not in civilian clothes, you won't. We'll swap," said Gus. "They'll just take you for an airman and put you back in a POW camp. Sorry, Duncan."

"And the Cadots? The Germans will accuse them of hiding me. You go while you can. I'll take my chances here."

"Gus, we can't leave Duncan!" exclaimed Eunice.

"We're not going to leave him," said Gus. "What I've got in mind is a tad risky and might not work. But if you are captured in my uniform, you'll get hospital treatment."

"I'll do it, then," agreed Duncan.

"What's the plan?" asked Eunice.

"You, Baudouin and Claude need to get going right now. Find the British soldiers and get down to the beach with them. Eunice, you must persuade them to take the three of you back to Blighty by boat."

"All right. What about you?"

"I'll swap clothing with Duncan then get the car. I'll come back for you, Duncan. Then we'll go home in style. We're going to fly!"

As he finished speaking, a gigantic explosion shook the cellar. They all scrambled up the steps, making their way to the surface. The sky was almost light. Flames and a great plume of smoke rose from the gun battery to the east.

"Which way?" asked Eunice.

Baudouin pointed along a lane. "That way leads to the sea, but be careful. We could be killed by English or German soldiers in this confusion."

They hadn't gone more than two hundred yards before the sound of boots on the track came from behind them.

"Take cover," whispered Eunice, and they quickly hid in some bushes at the side of the lane. Soldiers emerged. They were dressed in khaki and woollen hats, and Eunice noticed the British weapons they carried, a mix of Sten guns and Lee Enfield rifles.

"Hello. Don't shoot," called Baudouin from his cover.

The soldiers stopped and pointed their rifles. "Who are you?" shouted a corporal.

"French. We need to get away."

"Come out so we can see you, and keep your hands above your heads," said the corporal. "How many of you are there?"

Baudouin came out first. "There are three of us. Come on out," he said to the others. Claude and Eunice emerged from the bushes, arms held high. "We are all unarmed, *monsieur*," said Baudouin.

The soldiers lowered their rifles. "We've no room on the boats for you lot. You'd better go back inside and shut the doors."

"No, *monsieur*. We are being hunted by the Gestapo and will be killed."

Eunice drew a breath. "Lance-corporal," she said, in her cut-glass English accent. "My name is Eunice Hesketh and I'm a British agent. With me are two French Resistance fighters. We must get away. I insist that you take us immediately to the officer commanding your unit."

The commando started. "Yes, miss. This way, then. We've boats down at the beach waiting for us."

The three visibly relaxed. "Hold on," said Eunice. "Do you have any morphine?"

"Yes, I do."

"Quickly, hand me some. There's a badly wounded British officer back there."

The corporal found a first aid pouch in his pocket and handed it to Eunice.

"I'll be two minutes," she said. "One of you wait for me."

"I'll come with you, miss," said the lance-corporal, "if that's all right?"

"Yes, that's fine. Come along then, no time to lose."

CHAPTER 32

Gus watched Eunice and the commando trot back along the lane to the beach. Once they were out of sight, he turned the other way and went to look for the Citroën. He soon found it, and drove back to the *pigeonnier*. Duncan was waiting outside. There was nobody around to see him. Their French hosts were clearly inside, keeping as safe as possible. There were no British soldiers to be seen, and Gus guessed that the Germans were either dead or injured from the explosion, or were down on the beaches and cliffs, shooting at the escaping raiding force.

"Right, let's get you in the car," he said.

Duncan was drowsy from the shot of morphine that Eunice had given him a few moments before. Gus knew it wouldn't stop the pain completely, but it would deaden it enough for Duncan to move around a little.

With help from Gus, Duncan got onto the rear bench seat of the Citroën and shut the door. Then Gus got into the driver's seat and off they drove.

"Gus, if I could read your mind, I'd say you suspect Grindlethorpe of blowing the mission," said Duncan.

"I'm not sure about that," Gus replied.

"If he did, then he's responsible for the Gestapo getting Monique. We were…"

"I know. Eunice told me."

"They'll torture her, you know. They can be unbelievably cruel. I'll kill that bastard Grindlethorpe if he betrayed us!"

"Calm down, Duncan. It's much more likely that the local Gestapo got lucky."

"Really? I suppose so. Oh, and Gus…"

"Yes?"

"Thanks for this, pal. For staying with me and trying to get us out."

"No need to thank me. I'm a pilot — I was born to fly."

When Gus and Duncan reached the airfield, they found it deserted.

Gus looked around and spotted three aeroplanes: an Fw-190, a three-engined Junkers Ju-52, and a Blohm and Voss BV-141 reconnaissance plane. The Focke-Wulf could probably outrun any Allied fighter sent to intercept it, but it only had one seat, and Duncan was too badly injured to double up in it on a cross-Channel flight.

"We'll take that one," said Gus, pointing at the Blohm and Voss, "so long as it's got petrol in it. I'd rather start up one engine than three."

The BV-141 was an odd-looking aircraft. Designed for maximum observer visibility, its glazed crew gondola was offset to the starboard side, whilst the fuselage on the port side led smoothly from the large BMW radial engine to an asymmetrical tail unit.

"You sure you can fly it, Gus?" asked Duncan.

"I should think so. One kite's pretty much like another, and we're not going to be doing any aerobatics."

Gus privately wondered if he would be able to master the unfamiliar controls. Leaving Duncan in the Citroën, he went to check the German plane had fuel in it. When he opened the fuel cap, he could see and smell petrol. Good.

He went back to the car and drove it as close to the Blohm and Voss as he could. "Look, Duncan, this is going to hurt, but we've got to get you into that cockpit," he said. "Once we're in, there'll be loads of space. It looks like it's designed for a three-man crew, so you'll have lots of room to put your feet up and relax. Ready?"

Duncan sweated and swore his way from the Citroën, over a patch of grass and up a ladder, which took him inside the BV-141's glazed gondola. Once in, he collapsed.

Gus looked at the controls. He thought of a Westland Lysander's tail trim wheel. Was there anything similar on the Blohm and Voss? He had no way of knowing. He'd just have to assume that the last Luftwaffe pilot to fly it had the kite all set up for take-off.

Gus had a plan in mind. He'd fly at low level, head to the west of any smoke and find the French coast. Then he'd turn to starboard and pick up a course due north, which would bring him to the English coast. Once he could see it, he'd head away from any urban areas and airfields, as that was where ack-ack would come from. Then he'd pancake the German kite and wait for a policeman or the Home Guard to come and get him and Duncan.

"Sit tight, Duncan. I'm going to remove the chocks then have a go at starting the engine."

"Off you go, old boy. Take as long as you like. I'm feeling drowsy and want to try to get a bit of sleep."

Gus went to the first wheel of the aeroplane and stooped down to get rid of the chock. He heard voices over to the left. Germans. Bugger. He backed off to the right of the reconnaissance aircraft and lay flat on the floor under the Focke-Wulf, well away from the Luftwaffe guards. With everything that was happening in the town and on the beaches, these men would be on full alert and probably trigger-happy. With a bit of luck, they'd walk on and let Gus get on with the job of escaping.

Suddenly there was a scream from inside the BV-141. *Oh no*, thought Gus. *Duncan must have moved in his half-sleep and jarred his leg.* Immediately the guards were alerted. Gus saw torchlights shine onto the Blohm and Voss. He glimpsed rifles pointing towards the aeroplane and heard the challenges shouted. The guards were all gazing towards the reconnaissance aircraft.

There was nothing Gus could do to help Duncan. The Germans would find a wounded British airman and take him prisoner, for the second time in two years.

But the commotion gave Gus a chance. He removed the chocks on the Fw-190 and stealthily climbed into the cockpit, where he made himself as inconspicuous as possible and waited.

He could hear some of what was going on over by the BV-141. Gus knew Duncan spoke excellent German and with any luck he would shout out a surrender and tell them he was badly injured. They probably had an ambulance. It would drive out, take at least ten minutes to get Duncan stabilised and out of the cockpit, and then take him to the base buildings or field hospital.

While all this was going on, Gus wracked his brain. What had Staś told him about the captured 190? Wasn't it the easiest modern German aircraft to start up alone unaided? Listening to the sound of a light motor vehicle approaching the Blohm and Voss, Gus searched his memory.

Make sure the petrol tap is on — *obvious*, he thought. Ah, yes. He'd need to give it half a dozen pumps on the doper. He looked for anything resembling a hand-pump and found it. He then quickly located the starter switch. Was it down to charge and up to engage? Or was it the other way round? If he got this wrong, the false start would be heard all over the base. Or would it? The noise of the battle down at the beaches seemed to be livening up. Maybe the Navy was trying to give the departing boats some cover.

He waited until the vehicle had driven off, then gave it ten more minutes. Eventually, Gus carefully raised his head to look around. Nothing. Nobody. It was now or never.

He took a deep breath, held the starter switch down and counted to fifteen. Then, more slowly, he counted to five. He lifted the switch and the engine engaged first time.

A guard shouted a challenge. "Is that you, Oberleutnant Lechner?"

Gus took the safety catch off his revolver.

The guard came closer and shone his torch up, into the cockpit. Gus saw the expression on the guard's face change as he spotted the civilian clothes. The guard raised his rifle as Gus fired. "Sorry," he said, "but that really was your own fault."

Gus pushed the stick forward and taxied, as quickly as he could without the tail lifting, to the leeward end of the strip. With the brakes on hard, Gus pushed forward on the throttle lever with his left hand to open up the powerful 14-cylinder BMW radial engine. The German plane began to move, just as some figures emerged from the buildings and ran at him, shouting. No shots were fired. Gus guessed that nobody on the ground could be sure it wasn't a German pilot going up.

Gus ignored them. With beads of sweat on his brow, he sent the plane rattling unsteadily along the grassy strip as he struggled with the unfamiliar controls. He was worried. What was the stall speed of the Fw-190? Was he going fast enough to get into the air? He thought so. He'd done this sort of thing before, and it felt right this time. Gus pulled back on the control column and the aeroplane nosed upwards. He was back in the air, easily clearing a small group of buildings in a neighbouring field.

The Fw-190 was airborne and heading due west, into wind. He glanced at the fuel gauge; it showed full. The previous pilot must have landed to re-fuel. Good. He decided to stay on a westerly course until he could pick up the Cherbourg Peninsula, then head north to the English coast. That ought to get him somewhere between Portsmouth and Chichester. He might even make Tangmere. But he didn't care; he just wanted to get home. He thought that most aerial activity would be at mid to high altitudes and decided to keep low. In any case, he didn't have an oxygen mask. He'd keep low, get to Blighty, then put her down in the drink — it didn't matter.

It was then that Gus saw the Hurricanes. *Bugger*, he thought. *I get this far only to be shot up by the bloody RAF.* But the British fighters didn't open fire. They must have been out of ammo. They tailed him, no doubt putting out a call on their RTs, reporting his position. When this had happened in Greece and he'd been intercepted by Gloster Gladiators whilst escaping in an Italian bomber, Gus had flung back the cockpit canopy and let loose a white sheet, having tied one corner of it onto a sturdy piece of cockpit. No such luxury here. What could he do? He slowed down, opened the cockpit and waved frantically at the leading Hurricane. He was flying without any headgear and was wearing a civilian suit, but would the Hurricane pilot be able to make this out? Probably not.

Gus waggled the wingtips of the German aeroplane and waved again.

The leading Hurricane came abreast of him on the port side. Its cockpit canopy was flung back and the pilot gave him the thumbs-up. *Thank goodness*, thought Gus. *Even if they don't recognise me as English, at least they know I mean no harm.*

Escorted by the flight of Hurricanes, Gus landed the Fw-190 on the familiar strip at RAF Tangmere. He pushed the cockpit cover fully open and climbed down from the Focke-Wulf. Walking towards the oncoming ground crew, he turned back to look at the German fighter plane. He stared disbelievingly at the odd markings on it. In addition to the usual black crosses and swastikas, below the cockpit was a bright blue roundel with a *fasces* — a brown-handled axe with a silvery-white blade. Italian markings, exactly like the symbol his cousin Staś had described to him. Could this be the same Fw-190 that Staś had encountered? The same Butcherbird?

CHAPTER 33

Gus, Eunice and Peacock were gathered in the offices of 64 Baker Street.

"Thanks for coming," said Peacock, "and I'm sorry you had to leave DuncanFarquhar behind. Was he badly injured?"

"Broken leg," said Gus. "It'll heal, but there was no way he could have made it to the beach."

"And he couldn't make it to the aeroplane?"

"He did make it, but was rumbled by the Jerries. I feel so bloody guilty about leaving him there."

"It's not your fault, Gus," said Eunice.

"Quite," said Peacock. "Well, Operation Jubilee was a bloody disaster, wasn't it?"

"It seemed so from where we were, but I don't think we know the actual scale of it, Sir Alex."

"Then I'll tell you, but this is secret information, you understand. The British commandos you came off with —" Peacock looked at Eunice — "were Lord Lovat's men, and they had the only real success of the whole show when they put out those German guns. Two hundred and forty-seven of our commandos have been lost from a force of about a thousand men. Of the fifty US Army Rangers serving in commando units, six were killed, seven wounded and four captured. The Canadians took a real beating. Out of nearly five thousand of them, we believe three thousand three hundred have been lost — killed, wounded or taken prisoner. And we lost all of the tanks, about fifty of them."

"Bloody hell!" exclaimed Gus.

"They were brand-new Churchill tanks, and now the blasted Jerries know all about them. And it gets worse. The Royal Navy lost the destroyer HMS *Berkeley* and thirty-three landing craft. They have about five hundred and fifty sailors dead or wounded. The RAF has lost over a hundred aircraft. Among these losses, six aircraft were shot down by our own gunners; one Hawker Typhoon was shot down by a Spitfire. Two other Typhoons were lost when their tails broke off, which doesn't bode well for their future. Two Spitfires collided during the withdrawal across the Channel."

"Did the Germans know we were coming?" asked Gus.

"To be perfectly frank, Gustaw, we're not sure. On the seventeenth of August, the clue 'French port' appeared in the *Daily Telegraph* crossword. The next day, on the eighteenth, the solution 'Dieppe' was published. As you know, the raid on Dieppe took place the following day, the nineteenth. Some in the War Office suspect that the crossword was used to pass intelligence to the Germans. Johnnie Buchan is looking into it, but I doubt he'll find anything. Since June, the BBC has been broadcasting warnings to French civilians of a 'likely' action, urging them to evacuate the Atlantic coastal districts. Indeed, on the day of the raid itself, the BBC announced it, albeit at eight o'clock in the morning, after the Dieppe landings had taken place."

"What about the Resistance's report? The cell in Dieppe insists it sent a copy over to us," said Eunice.

"Nothing was received in my office."

"The leader of the cell was quite clear. He told us that one copy of the report — the typed original, in fact — was picked up by a Lysander. He said this was a month before we landed."

"Nothing got through to me," said Peacock. "What about the other copies?"

"The carbon copy was smuggled out by a less certain route. It should have been received in England by now," said Eunice.

"I can understand how the carbon copy might have stumbled," said Gus, "but if the original was picked up by a Lizzie, why didn't it get through?"

The look on Wing Commander Peacock's face was grave. "There's only one possibility. Someone intercepted it. That person is deliberately concealing information from me. And there is only one other person who might have met that Lysander."

Gus nodded grimly. "Squadron Leader Titus Grindlethorpe."

Gus and Eunice left Baker Street and stretched their legs on the brisk thirty-minute walk to Soho, where they popped into their usual tearoom off Greek Street.

Peering at Gus over her cup, Eunice asked, "Do you think Grindlethorpe is a traitor?"

"It's not the first time I've been asked that question."

"Really?"

"Peacock asked me. It was after Operation Lodz. Lodz was a mission to drop Polish agents into Poland. It was a disaster. The Joes were shot up as soon as they landed, and seven of the people on the ground were killed too. I was navigator and in on the debrief. Squadron Leader Krawiec, Polish SOE, was convinced that somebody here in London tipped off the Germans. And his money was on Grindlethorpe. So, when it was just me and Peacock in the room, the wing commander asked me if I thought Squadron Leader Grindlethorpe was a traitor."

"And?"

"I said I didn't think he was. I told Peacock that Squadron Leader Krawiec must be wrong. Nobody in London had tipped off the Germans. It was one of the Resistance's own — perhaps one of them was captured and tortured, or did it deliberately, for money. But I genuinely didn't believe that a tip-off had come from this end."

"And what do you think now, Gus?"

"I'm not sure what I think, Eunice. It seems like there must be a traitor at this end. So, yes, it could be Grindlethorpe, I suppose. Let's leave it to Sir Alex, shall we? Talk about something else?"

"Well, you'll be pleased to know that Baudouin and Claude are safe in England — Peacock has put them up somewhere secure. They'll probably work for him directly for now. And I could tell you about the sailor who took us off that beach and put us on the ship in Dieppe."

"Handsome, was he?"

"Sort of. He was a male version of our friend Milly Turner, actually. He turned out to be her brother, Harry."

"What? You must be joking."

"No, I'm deadly serious. Harry Turner was manning the landing craft that took us off the beach."

"I've just got to hear this," said Gus, topping up their teacups.

"The soldiers took us down to the beach. Orange Beach, they called it. There were a number of landing craft waiting, and the soldiers helped me and the others onto the first one. A young sailor grabbed my arm and said, 'C'mon, we'll soon have you in the warm and dry.' His voice reminded me of Milly straight away; then, as we neared the bigger boat, I looked up at his face. He looked so much like her."

"Did you get to talk to him at all?"

"Later, on the ship as we steamed back to England. He and another sailor brought mugs of tea around. I asked him his name. 'Harry,' he said. 'Harry Turner.' And I said, 'You're from Salford, aren't you?' He looked at me, flabbergasted, and nodded. I told him I knew his sister, Milly. Then we sat down for a longer chat.

"Harry was badly shaken by the raid. He told me he'd started the day transporting a platoon of Canadian soldiers onto a different beach — Green Beach. The landing was running late. At about half past two, as the craft were lowered into the water, one of the escort vessels moved off station, bringing some boats with it into the wrong place and causing a delay. They were late. Harry saw a star-shell burst in the dark sky to the east of them, and his mate Bob said it looked like some of our boys had been rumbled. Harry glanced at his watch as the sound of gunfire erupted on the left-hand side of the landing craft flotilla. The Canadians in the landing craft were spooked by it, and Harry told them to keep their heads down. He shouted to the soldiers in his boat that the firing was miles away and wasn't going to touch them. Then he chatted with them to calm their nerves. One Canadian soldier he particularly remembered was called Doug. Harry had thanked him for crossing the ocean to help the British."

"He's right. The Canadians didn't have to join the war, did they?"

"I've never really thought about it. Anyway, Harry said the noise increased and the exchange of gunfire to the east lit up the sky. Then a huge white flare rose from the shore and soared high. He knew that all chance of surprise for the Canadians had gone. Harry looked towards the beach; it was now less than fifty yards ahead of them. There were landing craft to his left and right. He saw a ten-foot stone sea wall topped with barbed wire about twenty yards across the beach. He said that nobody had warned them of that…"

"Because Grindlethorpe intercepted the bloody report."

"We can't be sure of that. Not yet. Anyway, the beach was quiet and looked deserted; maybe they would be all right after all. Then there was an order: 'Prepare to stand!' Harry said the men looked afraid, and some fidgeted with their equipment. There was a terrific crunching sound as the flat-bottomed craft crashed into the pebble beach. Someone shouted to lower the bow door. And the Canadians stood as bullets pinged furiously off the landing-craft door as it clattered down onto the beach. The lieutenant and sergeant were first out of the landing craft, charging onto the beach, followed by the young soldiers. Then the German machine guns opened fire in earnest, sending bodies crashing onto the pebbles a couple of yards in front of the bow door. Harry said he flinched and ducked instinctively as a hail of bullets hit the side of the boat. Soldiers leaped out of the landing craft, jumped over the bodies of their comrades and fell on the beach between the landing craft and the sea wall. Harry saw that a few of the Canadians had made it to the wall, but it was far too high to climb. But at least it sheltered them from the bullets that were raining over their heads and hitting those of their comrades who were still disembarking from the landing craft.

"Harry could see the soldiers were completely unaware of the strength of the German defences. He said he was frozen, looking at the death and destruction in front of him. Then he heard Bob shouting at him to raise the door and pull back. Harry raised the landing craft's door as the boat slammed into reverse. As they turned around and sailed away from the shore, the German gunners lost interest in them. Harry saw wounded men floating in the sea. He shouted at the helmsman to slow down. He thought he could retrieve one of them. He took a boathook and reached for a soldier, who was floating face-up.

He hooked the man's knapsack straps and pulled him closer, then got a good view of the soldier's face. It was Doug, the Canadian he'd thanked only minutes before. He was dead, his chest ripped apart by German bullets. Harry said he let Doug's body fall back into the water and shouted to the helm to get going."

"No bloody wonder poor Harry was badly shaken up. Sounds dreadful."

"It was dreadful," said Eunice. "Anyway, after that the craft were blown off course, and he ended up with the commandos on Orange Beach."

CHAPTER 34

A few weeks later, Gus received the news that Staś Rosen had been fished, unconscious, from the sea off Dieppe and taken back to England. He had been in a coma for two weeks, which he had now come out of with a degree of memory loss. Of course, his squadron had been advised of this, but nobody had thought to let Gus know.

Eventually, Gus received a letter from Staś himself. In it, Staś explained that he was recovering in the Palace Hotel in Babbacombe, the same RAF officers' hospital Gus had been in. With Peacock's assistance, Gus and Eunice managed to get some time off to travel down to the West Country to visit him.

"Well," said Gus, "I'm not surprised nobody told me you'd survived. I'm hardly next of kin, am I?"

"Actually, you might be," answered Staś.

"Sorry, I wasn't thinking. Come on, tell me the story."

"We were escorting a flight of Bostons over to Dieppe when we were bounced by a squadron of Fw-190s. I say a squadron, but there seemed to be hundreds of them. Well, they attacked the bombers first, of course, and then we dived on the Focke-Wulfs. It was mayhem. One of the bastards shot up Lech Lewandowski's Spitfire then killed poor Lech in cold blood as he hung from his parachute. It was just like Tunio all over again, Gus. It was awful.

"Well, I sought that bastard out and found him. Then I attacked. The two of us whirled around, performing the opposite loops of a figure of eight, but the Focke-Wulf was gaining on me. Time was running out. I had one thing in my favour. One tiny advantage, and a slim one at that. We all know a Butcherbird can outperform the Spitfire V that I was piloting, but not a Spitfire IX."

Gus nodded. He knew that with its improved Merlin 66 engine, the Spitfire IX had a top speed of four hundred and four miles per hour, thirty-three miles per hour faster than the Spitfire V. This would match the Fw-190.

"But — and this is the point — the two Spits look almost identical, especially at a glance in a dogfight," Staś went on. "That Nazi pilot wouldn't know whether I was flying a V or IX model Spit. This would put a tiny seed of doubt into this mind, slow his decision-making for a split second. At least, that is what I hoped for.

"Stick over and well forward, I plunged the Spitfire into a dangerous, near-vertical dive. At ground level I pulled into another steep turn, weaving and dodging the taller buildings of Dieppe as well as the columns of smoke. It was awful down there. I caught glimpses of the promenade, littered with British tanks, one or two moving but most of them stationary. I saw the white casino and the beach beyond it, filled with the bodies of Allied soldiers.

"The Fw-190 was still tailing me, but now came the time to throw him off. I'd spotted a destroyer surrounded by a clutter of smaller boats a short distance offshore. We'd been briefed not to fly over shipping at less than four thousand feet. Below this height, the destroyer would open fire. I put my trust in the slowness of Royal Navy gunners."

"And were you right to do so?"

"I was. I rammed the throttle into the emergency position, broke off my turn and headed straight for the destroyer at sea level. I glanced at the mirror and caught a glimpse of the Fw-190 right behind me. Then I pulled back on the stick as hard as I possibly could. The Merlin was screaming as I put the Spitfire into a vertical climb, the first part of a loop-the-loop. As I turned upside-down, I rolled her over and entered the dive, facing the Focke-Wulf, which was now five hundred feet below me. The German was heading east. He'd given up; maybe he was out of ammunition. Perhaps he'd taken a hit from the destroyer's flak — I don't know. I checked the fuel level. It wasn't too good, but enough for one more go at him, and I knew I had plenty of ammunition for the Brownings.

"I had the Focke-Wulf in my sights now. It was definitely the Italian, the same Nazi pilot that had killed Lech Lewandowski in cold blood. I wasn't going to let the brute escape. As the Fw-190 swerved and twisted at sea level, I stuck to it like glue. I was awaiting my opportunity for a good, long burst from the four .303 Browning machine-guns and two Hispano 20mm cannons. Eventually it came. I don't know whether the pilot was tired or wounded, but he made a mistake. Again he turned to the left, but this time his turn was too shallow. It gave me the chance to let off a burst at the port side of the Focke-Wulf. I pressed the fire button on the stick. The Spitfire shook violently as the guns and cannons discharged a short burst into the Focke-Wulf. That's the bastard finished, I thought, but no. He got away. I decided my fuel was low and turned to head for home. It was then that I was bounced by two more Focke-Wulfs and shot down into the bloody Channel."

"Staś, that Fw-190, the one with the Italian markings, you're not going to believe this, but I pinched it and flew back to Blighty in it."

"What?"

"It's true, unless there are more than one of them." Gus related the story of his escape to Staś.

"Well, I never. You seem to be making a habit of stealing enemy planes and hitching rides in them. Any other news to tell?"

"Yes, as a matter of fact." Gus looked at Eunice. "I've asked Eunice to marry me, and she's said yes. Staś, will you be my best man?"

HISTORICAL NOTES

CHARACTERS AND PERSONALITIES

My uncle, Harry Turner, fought what some might call a 'lucky' war.

After initial training in the Royal Navy, Harry was posted to HMS *Hood* along with his pal, Johnny Cole. Both were Salford lads. Harry was pulled in for drunkenness and fighting by the provosts the night before *Hood* sailed on her final, fateful voyage. He was slung into a cell and when he awoke the next day, *Hood* had sailed to intercept the German battleship *Bismarck*. HMS *Hood* sank on 24 May 1941, having been hit by shells from *Bismarck*, with the loss of 1,415 men. Only three of her crew survived. One of those killed was John Henry Cole; aged eighteen, Johnny was the son of Mark and Eliza Cole, of Salford. The loss of what had been considered an invincible warship badly affected British morale.

Later, Harry volunteered for Combined Operations and took part in the raid on Dieppe (1942), crewing a landing craft. I have little idea of which beach Uncle Harry landed on. It was unlikely to be Orange, where there were few casualties. My idea of him starting on Green Beach and being blown onto Orange Beach later in the morning is a fiction.

My mother described her brother as being 'a bag of nerves' for years afterwards. She related to me the story of Harry casting aside the body of a soldier and, months later, seeing the same man alive and well. As a child, I took this piece of family folklore at face value. A mistake in the heat of battle. A soldier thought dead, who lived to tell the tale. As an adult, I now believe it more likely that Harry was suffering the effects of what modern doctors would probably diagnose as post-traumatic stress disorder.

Wing Commander Sir Alexander Peacock is entirely fictitious, though I expect military types like him were scattered all over wartime London. Peacock recruits Gus Beaumont for service in the Special Operations Executive (SOE). The SOE was formed in 1940 from the amalgamation of three existing secret organisations (MI6, the Electra House Department, and MI(R), the guerrilla warfare research department of the War Office). The purpose of the SOE was to conduct reconnaissance, espionage and sabotage against the Axis powers in occupied Europe, and to aid local resistance movements.

Lord Louis Mountbatten, known as Dickie, was made Acting Vice Admiral and Head of Combined Operations by Churchill in early 1942.

Archie Rafferty need not have worried about the lack of activity for the Royal Scots Fusiliers. In May 1942 the first and second battalion of that regiment fought together in relieving Madagascar from the Vichy French forces.

Gordon Cummins, the Blackout Killer, murdered four women and attempted to murder two others in London over a six-day period in February 1942. He was convicted in April and hanged at Wandsworth Prison in June that year.

Johnnie Buchan (John Norman Stuart Buchan, 2nd Baron Tweedsmuir and son of the novelist, John Buchan) was a senior intelligence officer attached to the Canadian Army. He was asked to investigate the *Daily Telegraph* crossword issue and later said: "In the end, it was concluded that it was just a remarkable coincidence — a complete fluke."

Marc Bloch (1886–1944) was a French historian and member of the French Resistance. One of the names he went by was Chevreuse. Bloch joined the Resistance movement sometime between late 1942 and March 1943. He was executed by the Gestapo in 1944. Bloch also appears in the first two Gus Beaumont Aviation Thrillers, *Bouncer's Battle* and *Bouncer's Blenheim*.

PLACES

Audley End House in Essex was used as a general holding camp for the SOE, eventually becoming the base of a Polish branch. The Polish SOE War Memorial in the main drive commemorates one hundred and five Polish SOE personnel who died in World War Two. A full account of one particular Polish section SOE operation is to be found in Jeffrey Bines' *Operation Freston: The British Military Mission to Poland, 1944* (1999).

Bunty Kermode's role at Bletchley Park was in the Boniface section of Ultra, the designation adopted by British military intelligence for wartime signals intelligence. So keen was British intelligence to ensure Germany should not know Bletchley Park was cracking its codes, that it created a fictional MI6 master spy, Boniface. If the Germans could be convinced that Boniface existed and controlled a series of agents throughout Germany, then information obtained through codebreaking could be attributed to the human intelligence gained through the Boniface network. Bunty, and a team of similarly trained young women, spent their days sending and receiving messages to this phantom network, but they had no idea that Boniface and his network was entirely fictitious. Few were allowed to know. Most government officials and British naval officers believed the vital information was coming from an MI6 master spy and his network of agents.

Sadly, it turned out that RAF Hospital Torquay was not safe from attack. On Sunday, 25 October 1942, the hospital was attacked by enemy Jabos (probably Fw-190s). Eyewitnesses reported seeing enemy aircraft approaching the hospital from low over the sea, followed by machine-gun fire and two loud explosions. One bomb scored a direct hit on the hospital, leaving a trail of death and destruction.

MISSIONS AND OPERATIONS

The success of Operation Archery, also known as the Måløy Raid, in December 1941 was sufficient to persuade Adolf Hitler to divert thirty-thousand troops to Norway and to build more coastal and inland defences.

The idea for my chapter on Operation Lodz is loosely based on Jeffrey Bines' account of Operation Freston, though Karol Błaszczykowski's emergency landing of the Halifax is based on RAF pilot Andrew Wilson's action in landing a badly damaged Halifax following a mid-air collision over France. The real Jozef Dubiel was my daughter-in-law's grandfather. He was an air-gunner with the RAF/Polish SOE, fighting in both Wellington and Halifax bombers. Having escaped from Poland in 1939, Jozef went on to be awarded the Order of Virtuti Militari: Poland's highest military decoration for heroism and courage in the face of the enemy at war. He remained in the UK after 1945.

Operation Millennium, the thousand-plane bombing raid on Cologne on 30 May 1942, killed 469 people and left 45,000 homeless.

There has been much debate over the merits or otherwise of Operation Jubilee, the Dieppe Raid. A good overview of the background and execution of Operation Jubilee from one who considers the operation to be a disaster can be found in Patrick Bishop's book *Operation Jubilee, Dieppe 1942: The Folly and the Sacrifice* (1997).

For detail of the aerial operations which formed part of Operation Jubilee, see Norman Franks' *The Greatest Air Battle: Dieppe, 19th August 1942* (1997).

There was an organised French Resistance group around Dieppe which produced a comprehensive report on German defences. This aided the success of Operation Biting (a Combined Ops raid on the German coastal radar installation at Bruneval). Patrick Bishop's *Operation Jubilee* states that in March 1942 a French agent called 'Dutertre' visited the area, where he met local sympathisers and spent two weeks collecting evidence of gun positions, etc. On 25 March, Dutertre left for Paris with the dossier but missed the handover to agent 'Pol', who was to take it to the UK. Another handover was arranged for two weeks later, but Pol was arrested before it took place. The dossier of vital information eventually reached London in late August.

The Cadot family encountered commandos in the lanes around Vasterival before taking shelter in the cellar beneath the *pigeonnier*. The cartridges on which eleven-year-old Gérard Cadot burned his fingers are thought to have come from British aeroplanes.

AIRCRAFT, TANKS AND TACTICS

The Focke-Wulf Fw-190 could out-perform a Supermarine Spitfire V in most areas. For example, it had a top speed of 405mph compared to the Spitfire's 370mph and a rate of climb of 3,000 feet/second (c/f 2,600 ft/sec).

An 'Italian' Fw-190, such as that purloined by Gus for his escape, was spotted by Squadron Leader George Leonard 'Johnny' Johnson and is quoted by Norman Franks in *The Greatest Air Battle: Dieppe, 19th August 1942* (1997).

On 23 June 1942 Oberleutnant Armin Faber landed his Fw-190 at RAF Pembrey, Carmarthenshire. Afterwards, upon realising his mistake, the devastated Faber attempted suicide. The aeroplane was immediately sent to the Royal Aircraft Establishment, Farnborough, repainted with British markings and flown to the Air Fighting Development Unit at Duxford for tests.

Adapted Westland Lysanders were used to drop and pick up SOE agents and supplies. Full accounts of these operations are to be found in Hugh Verity's *We Landed by Moonlight*, Crecy Publishing (1998).

Some bombers were converted for SOE and other covert operations. A hole was cut in the fuselage for the agents to exit through. To the flight crews, all SOE agents, men and women alike, were known as 'Joes', hence the 'Joe hole' in Chapter 9.

I have taken the liberty of having Gus pilot a Lockheed Hudson in the summer of 1942. The SOE did use Hudsons, but Hugh Verity reports that the first SOE operational flight in one was not until January 1943.

Fighter-bombers were known to the Luftwaffe as Jabos. They had been tried by specialist Luftwaffe units such as *Erprobungsgruppe* 210 during the Battle of Britain, but these had generally been small and low-altitude sorties. The Jabos were not much of a tactical threat — apart from the specialists — as they were notoriously inaccurate when dropping their bombs. Nevertheless, against area targets such as London they could still cause significant damage and civilian deaths.

The first of the Jabo raids undertaken by Fw-190s was on 7 July 1942, I have them attacking Hastings a little earlier in that year. The method of Jabo attack I described was developed in 1941 by Oberleutnant Frank Liesendahl and known as the Liesendahl Process. But the use of fighters as fighter bombers was not universally accepted.

The instructions for starting a Fw-190 were found in the International Bomber Command Centre Digital Archive, University of Lincoln. At the time, the Fw-190 was indeed the easiest modern German aircraft to start up alone and unaided. I figured that an experienced pilot with enough German to read the instrument labelling — and, what's more, a lucky pilot, like Bouncer Beamont — might have a good chance of starting one up.

The account of Paddy O'Brian getting a Lysander stuck in a French field is based on Operation Scenery, November 1943, when Flight Lieutenant Robin Hooper could not extricate Lysander MA-D and spent a month in a safehouse.

There is still disagreement about how late the Royal Regiment of Canada was landed onto Blue Beach at Puys. Some accounts suggest it was only seventeen minutes. Others put it at thirty-five minutes for the first landings and up to an hour for all the troops to be landed.

Of the sixty Churchills detailed to land on Red and White Beaches, only the tanks of the first two waves were actually landed. The latter two waves were repulsed by heavy defending fire. Of those thirty tanks, one was trapped in its LCT by shellfire, two sank and eleven were immobilised on the beach. The rest got off the beach and over the seawall onto the Dieppe promenade.

SHIPS

HMS *Audacity* was a captured German merchant ship (the *Hanover*) that had been converted into a convoy escort carrier. She sailed to Gibraltar with Convoy OG 76, then back to the UK (with HG 76) carrying four serviceable Grumman Martlet fighters. Those fighters destroyed two Focke-Wulf Fw-200 Condors. HMS *Audacity* sank on the night of 21 December 1941 with the loss of seventy-three of her crew.

A NOTE TO THE READER

Dear Reader.

Thank you for taking the time to read *Bouncer's Butcherbird*. I hope you enjoyed reading it as much as I enjoyed writing it.

Reviews are invaluable to authors, so if you liked the book, I'd be grateful if you could leave a review on **Amazon** or **Goodreads**.

Readers can connect with me online **on Facebook** and **X (formerly Twitter)**.

I hope we meet again in Gus Beaumont's next adventure!

Tony Rea

Sapere Books is an exciting new publisher of brilliant fiction and popular history.

To find out more about our latest releases and our monthly bargain books visit our website:
saperebooks.com

Printed in Great Britain
by Amazon

54177502R00116